IDOLS & CONS

IDOLS & CONS

S. S. Michaels

Omnium Gatherum
Los Angeles CA

Idols & Cons
Copyright © 2011 S.S. Michaels
ISBN-13: 978-0615556437
ISBN-10: 0615556434

This book is a work of fiction. Names, characters, places and incidents are either the products of the author's imagination or are used fictitiously. Any resemblance to actual events or persons, living or dead, is coincidental

First Edition

This book is for my beautiful and brainy daughters, Sian and Emma, who may someday be allowed to read it. This book is also for my wonderful husband, Chazz, who made it possible for me to stay home and write to my heart's content. This book is for my friends and family, who lent me not only their critical eyes, but their support when I needed it. Thanks to my former employer, dick clark productions, inc., for giving me the opportunity to catch a glimpse of what boy bands are all about. Special thanks to my publisher, Kate Jonez, my proofreader, Molly Jones, and my favorite writing instructor and friend, Jeremy C. Shipp.

Fast-Forward

JAKE

Tuesday, October 31

As my vehicle glided to a halt, I checked the mirror one last time, ran a hand through my sticky brush cut. Totally unprepared for this battle, I steadied my breathing and assumed my calmest façade. I told myself there was no danger, no threat to my safety, not with this many witnesses. I pulled on my Revo shades, my Armani flak jacket. Zero hour. Deep breath. Smile. Let's do this.

A neutral party wearing a drive-thru headset and all black crept up to my door, jerked it open, and spoke my name into the bud of his microphone. Then, I was in it.

As soon as my Chuck Taylor touched the plush red runner, they were on me. An over-zealous firing squad on an AWOL private. Photographic assassins pointed their weapons, commanding my attention from all sides. The syndicate of snipers crouched along the red river, Nikon weapons poised and ready. Camera flashes ignited the violet vellum sky, fire from the muzzles of a hundred assault rifles. Celebrities, picked off in mid-lie, advanced from dark tinted personnel carriers to the neon-framed portal of Gallery 551.

The rush from a crack pipe hits you within seven seconds of inhalation. I can attest to that, first-hand. I can also tell you that's a freaking eternity compared to this.

"Jake, on your left!" *Flash.*

"Hey, Jake!" *Flash.*

"Smile, kid!" *Flash.*

"Hey, artist, to the right!" *Flash.*

Flash.

Flash.

Flash.

Surrounded, I was forced to surrender. I raised my hands above my head and submitted to their lenses with an air of resignation.

Okay, you got me.

I fucking loved it. I was blinded by the supernova flash bursts, but I loved it. Masses of people waved at me, jumping up and down, screaming from behind the phalanx of *paparazzi.* Not just people — fans! Blue and white floaters swam across my field of vision with every blink. Totally surreal. My head swelled with every squeal of my name. My anxiety dissolved to dizzy euphoria. It was beyond intense.

The celebrity high is instantaneous. Not even mainlining hits you that fast or hard. Heroin never felt as smooth. The world whirled around me in a slow motion hallucination of high powered admiration. My skin flushed with a warm tingle from my toes all the way to my scalp. My heart beat like the trance rhythm at an overcrowded rave, yet I felt calm, bordering on numb. I floated along on a sea of serene reverie. No needle required.

Through the glare of my brand new brilliance, I couldn't quite make out what she looked like, but I spotted this chick moving through the crowd. Her inky silhouette stalked me as I drifted across the savage firing range. A dull finger of concern dimpled the bubble of my ecstasy.

Flash.

She moved a beat faster than me. *Ah, just another photographer looking for a place to get a better shot. Don't sweat it,* I told myself. But I couldn't help sweating it. She moved with precision and purpose, searching for a particular location, predicting the trajectory of my forward motion. Maybe she wanted an autograph. Or my phone number. Sweet. I wondered if she was hot.

Flash.

"Hey, Jake, over here!" I snapped back to my surreal reality.

What the hell, they deserved it, these grunts with cameras. They'd probably been camped out on the sidewalk since early morning. I stopped and gave my best cooler-than-you sneer. I put my head on a slow right to left swivel, giving them all an equal opportunity to capture the money shot.

Flash, flash, flash.

They ate that shit right up.

Okay, so did I. It was a true symbiotic relationship, self-feeding, self-sustaining. I wished it could last forever.

An edge of dread bled through, though, damaging my high. I was no coward, but, well... *He* could be in there. Waiting for me just inside the door. Or in the bathroom, or something. I hadn't given it much thought until I saw that weird chick pacing me. I mean, security was pretty tight, so everything should be fine, but, still, I wasn't a hundred percent.

That chick, my harbinger of horror, perched at the bottom of the steps, right behind the velvet rope. She was a teenager, like me, maybe a year or two older. Damn, she wasn't hot. A bird's nest of frizzy yellow hair floated around her pudgy harsh face. The buttons down the front of her black shirt strained to contain the bloated mess within. I did not see a camera. Was that a dog collar around her neck?

The dog collar?

No way. Couldn't be — could it? Christ, I was freaking myself out. *Just a kid trying to get an eyeful. Get a grip, dickhead.* But I knew it was her — the girl I'd seen in my hotel room. The one who'd left me the letter. The cousin. The budding dread I'd felt before fully flowered in the pit of my stomach.

Flash.

I crept up to the velvet rope, struggling to maintain my celebrity swagger. The weird chick gripped a Starbucks cup in her porky fist. She pulled it back as flashbulbs reflected off the cup's cool white skin, glinted off her sparkly sapphire ring.

Flash.

Warm, thick, sticky liquid slapped my cheek, oozed down my neck, trailed down my leather jacket. It was not latte.

The chick disappeared.

My career was officially launched.

Hi.

Yeah, I'm him.

I know, you had my posters all over your bedroom and wrote my name over and over in your history notebook, right? You knew my middle name was William, my favorite color was blue, and that I drove a BMW motorcycle. You had all four of the shitty albums we made that first year, and your mom took you to six of our shows, bought you the fifty-dollar T-shirts and everything. You knew everything there was to know about me, yeah? Where are you from? The Valley, the O.C., maybe, like Mary? Definitely the 'burbs. I was your dream date, Ken to your Barbie.

Shit. That is so fucking funny.

I hate to tell you, but you got scammed. Everything was one hundred percent bullshit. Let me tell you something: you had no fucking idea what happened to me or where I came from. You only 'knew' me because of a fucked up, tripped out accident. I was there, in the spotlight, because Damien threw me under a bus. Nobody had any clue about what was really going on or where I suddenly came from. The media sank their professionally whitened fangs into me and made me an idol. And I played the game like a pro. I showed them all, didn't I? Beat them at their own game.

But, listen, I know none of it's your fault. You're the victim here, right? I'm just not what you think — I never was. You want the truth? You know what I was? A scared kid from the ghetto. They almost fucking killed me, you know. Oh, wait, that's right — they left that part out of the *Rolling Stone* interview.

Please, you don't want to meet me. You do not want to *know* me, the real me. I am too fucked up for you to even hold a conversation with. You can't save me. Or understand me, fix me, love me, whatever. So, please, don't approach me after shows. Don't pull at my clothes when I'm shopping for Oreos at Ralph's. Don't tell me how lucky I am. You don't know the half of it.

Yes, worship me, buy my records, my books, my videos, give me all your discretionary income, but just know that I have nothing more to say to you. I am damaged beyond repair. I'm an illusion. I am like a gorgeous facade on the scariest damned haunted house you could ever imagine.

I have been in solitary confinement since the night I saw it happen.

And I like it that way.

What? The news reports didn't sound that bad to you? You think I'm shitting you, giving you some bullshit rock star ego trip? Yeah, well, maybe I am.

But, deep down, you know I'm for real.

Barbie, I have seen levels of Hell not even Dante could imagine.

Christ.

I'm there right now.

Come on, I'll show you.

Flash.

JOHN

Friday, July 7

Damien snaked his fingers under the black dog collar and twisted it. The girl smiled and rode him harder, grinding her hips, tossing her head back. She guided his free hand up her ribcage, his fingers brushing her nipple before biting into the skin next to the shining rabies tag. Her smile grew wider and melted into a blurry mask of satisfaction. He bucked harder, bouncing her short black hair with every lurch.

A bead of sweat dropped out of my greasy day-glow yellow hair and clouded my eyepiece. I took a clumsy swipe at it with my left thumb. I remember wishing that they'd fix the air conditioning in my stupid building. Our landlord was such a freaking nub. I didn't want to miss a single second of this episode of the Damien Tungsten Show due to some idiotic temperature control issue. My right hand stroked up and down, up and down, faster and faster. I was so glad that douche bag didn't have curtains.

His hands wrenched the collar, forcing it downwards, threatening to break it. The hot little goth rode him like a pogo stick, mouthing 'oh' over and over again. I was so close to exploding. This was the hottest thing I'd seen in weeks.

The shit I usually got stuck with was Jabba the Nutjob in her see-through nightie, singing into a hair brush while clipping her toenails. Gag. Or Larry the Lawyer, in his perfectly organized Scandinavian bedroom, screaming into the CrackBerry that lived in the collapsed space between his ear and shoulder. I often wondered if that dude could even straighten his neck.

Oh, and sometimes, if I was really lucky, I caught a glimpse of Dee Dee Simone. In the raw. She was the same age as me, but she went to some fancy prep school in Beverly Hills. Typical 90210 type. Moved here with her parents from New York. Didn't even know I was alive, of course. Bitch. I should have told her that I liked the little rose tattoo on her ass.

Anyway, watching Damien nail this goth chick was beyond hot. I spit on my hand and pumped it faster, stroking myself right to the brink as Damien pulled her down onto all fours and knelt behind her. His hands yanked the collar tighter and tighter. The pace of my own ragged breathing doubled. More 'ohs' from her. As Damien slammed and banged away, the girl's chalky white face went red, then redder. Something didn't look right.

My hand dropped from my lap. I peered into my telescope, holding my breath. In seconds, the girl's complexion deepened to an alarming shade of purple.

Fuck. It's just the light or something. It has to be. I leaned back and shook my head. Maybe I'd just smoked too much weed. I bent over the scope. No. Something definitely wasn't right.

The wet gash of the girl's mouth spread into a grimace. Damien pumped away, completely oblivious. As usual.

He was choking her.

I couldn't do anything but watch and hope he'd realize what was happening.

Come on, come on, I pleaded, *look at her face.*

His eyes squeezed shut as his hips slowed, and he thrust harder as the collar pinched her windpipe shut. She lifted a hand toward her throat, mouth working frantically. She tried to lift her other hand, rearing up on her knees, but she was knocked off balance by Damien's every shudder. She touched his hands for half a second before her arms started flailing all over the place, grabbing for some unseen savior.

Oh my God.

At last, she flopped face down on the bed as Damien collapsed on top of her, never even glancing at her face.

Flash.

I backed away from the telescope for a minute, sweating and sick. Was that chick okay? Yeah, *pfft*, sure, she was fine. Damien had worked her pretty hard. She was exhausted, that was all. Yeah, just wrecked.

No, uh-uh, I wasn't convinced. I had never seen anyone that color before. Was that color even possible for human skin? It was like this tube of paint I bought a couple weeks ago for this killer sunset skull I had been painting. Some fucking long name, um, Quinacridone Red Violet, or something like that. Beautiful. For painting.

She could not have been that color, the last reasonable functioning synapse of my brain told me.

It had to have been the light.

I grabbed a brick of hash and a pipe from my nightstand and lit up. Trick of the light or not, I was seriously rattled. My hands shook so bad I could barely flick my Bic.

I slithered back to the telescope. Damien sat up, talking to the chick. I couldn't see much of her above the window frame. Maybe she was okay after all. Short-lived relief, drawn from the pipe, released some of the tension in my neck and jaw.

Damien shook the girl, like he was trying to wake her. Gently, smiling.

Then he shook her harder, his pinup smile drooping. Then, much harder.

Panic enlarged his eyes and cut lines around his sagging mouth.

It was like watching a house fire on a nanny cam.

I couldn't lie to myself any longer. I had watched it happen, for Christ's sake.

Damien killed that girl!

Holy shit.

I watched him jump out of bed and scuttle around the

room. He yelled at her. He raked his hands through his thick mop of dark hair and shouted, mouth stretched wide, eyes as big as hubcaps. Definitely not a picture he'd want on the cover of *J-14*.

I couldn't stand to look anymore.

But I had to see. Like driving by the scene of some horrible car wreck. What was he going to do? Could he wake her? I was totally riveted by the whole grisly scene.

I smoked some more while he pulled on his clothes and freaked out.

Full panic mode gripped him as he finally hauled her up off the bed and dragged her into the living room. I couldn't see whether he put her on the couch or the floor, not that it really mattered. He hurried back to the bedroom and got her clothes. Then, back into the living room. He disappeared beneath the window frame for a while. I don't know for how long, I was stoned beyond judging the passage of time at that point.

A while later — minutes, maybe twenty — much to my extreme horror and amazement, I watched the dude stumble out of his apartment building.

I rubbed my eyes in disbelief.

He lurched down the shallow concrete steps, where we normally sit and bullshit.

He half-carried, half-dragged a fat rolled up rug.

A frosty layer of sweat iced my naked back. A dream. Yeah, that was it, it was all a terrible dream. Or a hallucination — hash could do that to a person, right? I pushed the telescope out of the way so I could crouch under the window without being seen. I squeezed my eyes shut, shook my head, inhaled sharply, and looked outside.

No fucking way. He was still there. With the rug. Struggling down the steps.

I sunk to the floor, hoping like hell that he hadn't seen me, hoping that girl wasn't rolled up in that carpet, all blue and still.

Tell me she's not in there, Damien, I silently begged. Tell me you sent her home in a cab while I was passed out, and that everything's okay, and we can hang out on the steps tomorrow.

I'd done a lot of shitty stuff, but I never felt so dirty in my life. I wanted to take a shower and scrub my eyeballs with Lifebuoy soap on a nailbrush, but I was afraid my Mom would wake up. Taking a shower at two o'clock in the morning wasn't really part of my normal routine.

I grabbed the handset from the phone on my nightstand. I punched the 'talk' button and heard the dial tone. Wait, what was I doing? Calling the cops? Yeah, me, sitting in my room with a couple thousand dollars' worth of illegal drugs and a portable meth lab on my shabby old desk. Me, the 'peeping Tom' of Carson High. Me, the poor kid from the 'hood, making up stories about a rich and famous pop star.

I clicked the phone off and set it down. I sunk to the floor and rocked back and forth, knees pulled up to my chest. I thought about praying, but realized that I didn't know how. I looked around at my posters of The Ramones and The Damned, my cheap Picasso and Warhol prints. I pulled out a dime bag of heroin from the stash beneath my bed.

On second thought, ecstasy might be a better idea. Wouldn't totally wipe me out, but would still give me that 'everything's cool' feeling. I felt like I needed to be somewhat coherent. Why, I didn't know. I downed the pink tab with a swallow of Coke from a can that had been sitting on my desk for about four years.

I instantly felt a little calmer. Not much, but a little. Placebo effect. I knew it would take about half an hour for the genuine warm fuzzies to come on.

KELLY

Friday, July 7

He was the ugliest thing I'd ever seen. A Clumber spaniel, Aunt Donna told me. A purebred show dog. As if that butt-ugly thing could have ever won anything. He mostly followed my cousin Mary around, when he wasn't sleeping on the couch in a puddle of his own drool. Totally icky. He came wiggling down the hallway and plopped down right outside the open bathroom door. I could smell him from five feet away.

"Awww, who's a good boy?" Mary cooed at the fugly thing, rubbing his ear and wiping his goobery eye.

Like I said, totally icky, right?

"Hey," I interrupted, making a face at the dog's stringy eye boogers. "You think I should go with the blue eye-liner or the black?"

I stared in the mirror, studying the pink fleshy rim below my eyeball. My eyes were most definitely my best feature. Aside from my super-full, kissable lips, of course.

"Definitely black," she said, standing up and wiping eye boogers on a tissue. "Black goes with absolutely everything. Black is God."

Right, did I mention she was one of those pseudo-goth chicks? She was a year younger than me, but thought she was so much cooler because she only wore black and only listened to music they didn't play on the radio. The only reason she was going to the concert with me was because my mom guilted her mom into getting us tickets. Mary's mom, Aunt Donna, didn't ever let Mary go out and have any fun like a normal teenager. Well, that was according to my mom, who let me do whatever the hell I wanted and didn't give a dingo's dingle whether I was home by midnight or not. She didn't keep me in a cage like some purebred show dog.

Anyway, über-cool goth bitch, Mary, humored me by going along to the absolute biggest concert of the year, In Dreams' L.A. debut. At the Palladium in Hollywood, no less. I was so psyched that I'd barely slept since I'd arrived at her house the week before. I bought a bunch of new mags at the Denver airport on my way and memorized everything I could about Damien Tungsten. He was so beyond hot.

"Cute, sure, in a boring wholesome farm-boy way. But, you know," Mary said, pouting in the mirror, coloring her lips black, "he's probably gay."

I know, what a bitch, right? Well, we'll just see how totally not gay he is when we get backstage.

"We're going to meet him tonight," I said, touching up my own Candy Apple Red gloss. I looked amazing.

I saw her roll her eyes in the mirror. Disbeliever. She thought I was so stupid. But I wasn't. I knew how to get past security guys. I'd done it a few times back home. Last year, I got to meet Justin Bieber. It was beyond awesome. He even touched my hand. I wasn't going to wash it for a month, but my evil mother made me wash the dishes the next day.

Mary, lips perfectly black and disgusting, reached down to pet the slobbering dog thing. She pulled the black leather collar over his head and took off the I.D. tag. She couldn't get the rabies tag off, so she just left that on. Then, she buckled the thing around her neck and smirked at me. How lame, right? Ugh, she made me so totally ill.

Aunt Donna poked her head into the bathroom.

"Aren't you two over-doing it just a bit?" she said, scanning our make-up and jaw-dropping lacy outfits. "You're teenagers — you look twenty-five, both of you. I don't want any funny business tonight, you hear me? No drinking, no smoking, no anything."

Mary and I nodded. A giggle accidentally slipped through my lips. I couldn't help it. Damien Tungsten!

"Be back here right after the show, and I mean it. I know it's an hour away, but I'll give you two hours to be safe. I know what parking's like over there. That'll make it, what, about one o'clock?" She looked at us, eyebrows raised. "Remember, Kelly's got a flight in the morning."

She shouldn't have bothered worrying about that — I wouldn't make it anyway. Being the older, more responsible teen, I felt the need to reassure her.

"Don't worry, Aunt Donna," I said, "we'll be home way before then."

She gave me an unbelieving frown and walked out.

"Unless we meet some hot guys," I murmured to Mary.

Mary might be icky, but she was all for meeting boys, and she usually had plenty of them around. God knows why. She was all bony and ghostly. We giggled and Aunt Donna poked her head back in.

"I heard that. And, Mary," she said, "don't let your father see you looking like that."

Uncle James would so not approve of her outfit. He knew she always wore the typical goth make-up and clothes, and he'd made his peace with that, but her lacy teddy and micro skirt were totally not dad-friendly. Uncle James was due home from work at any minute, so we were in a rush to get out of there.

Mary sped us along the freeway in her mom's silver Mercedes SUV, some horrible scary music grinding out of all four hundred speakers. An hour later, I thought my head would explode as we pulled into a parking lot off of Hollywood Boulevard.

I'd been to Hollywood a couple of times before during my annual visits to Anaheim. It totally mesmerized me — the bright lights, the gorgeous people everywhere, that ginormous 'Hollywood' sign on the hill by the observatory. It was the exact opposite of the rural Colorado hellhole I'm from. Every year I went home and cried about how lucky stupid corpse-girl was. I desperately wanted to move there after high school, but there was no freaking way I could ever afford it. Maybe I'd get lucky and snag a scholarship to USC or UCLA or something. (Yeah, right. I was so not a student.)

But, as things turned out, I had to move there a whole lot sooner anyway. Yay for me.

When we got to the arena, there were people standing in line all over the place, mostly teenage girls. Snapping gum and texting, all of them. They were all way skinnier than me. Competition definitely looked tough. Shit.

The chicks that had to bring their moms stood a couple of feet away from the old crones, staring at their shoes and slowly dying of embarrassment. Mary and I joined the end of one line and, oh my God, someone's mom said 'hi' to us. It was so beyond gross.

My dazzling aquamarine eyes searched desperately for an escape. Blatantly ignoring the old lady's "where-are-you-girls-from?" blather, I spotted a heavily guarded gate in the chain link fence to the right of the arena's front doors.

"Hey," I whispered to Mary, tugging on her skeletal arm, "come on. We're going in."

I pulled her towards the gate, well away from the parental inquest. My too-cool cousin frowned and rolled her eyes at me. If I didn't get her out of there, we'd wind up talking to someone's mother about the weather or something for the next half hour.

Eeeww, I know, right?

Plus, I'd miss out on my destiny — meeting Damien.

We stepped up to the gate, pushing through a small mob of assorted skanks, and were greeted by a large hunk in a tight yellow 'security' polo and cop shades. Totally hot.

"Hi," I said to him. I shook my curly bleach-blonde hair

and smoothed the hem of my skirt. "My cousin and I are kind of with one of the roadies. We don't have passes or anything, but we met him at the Chateau bar last night, and he said to come find him at the show."

I batted my long black eyelashes and pursed my lips.

The security guy pulled off his sunglasses and studied my black cami and miniskirt. I could tell he was less than impressed.

Ouch, I know, right?

My face fell. I had to admit, though, next to the Hollywood skanks, I sincerely was kind of vomit inducing. I wasn't morbidly obese or anything, but I guess I was a smidge on the heavy side. But I had a dead gorgeous face. I thought. The security guy yawned at me. Damn, my one chance to meet Damien was slipping away.

"Yeah," Mary said, pushing up next to me, "he did say to meet him here. His name's Jerry, Larry, Terry... something erry."

She flashed a smoldering smile at the guard, who smiled back. He must go for those skinny slutty undead types. Pig. He looked back at me.

"Yeah, um, she's with him," I said, beaming, "but I'm available." Okay, not too smooth, but maybe he'd bite.

He sized up Mary, then gave me a cursory glance. He told us to wait a minute and walked over to a group of security guys who were standing in a circle, talking, on his side of the fence. After a minute or so, the guy came back with a replacement so he could escort us into the building.

It was working! We were getting in. I couldn't believe it. I smiled at Mary. She heaved a bored sigh and looked up at the purple sky. Jeez, some people.

We moved through a herd of stagehands who wore headsets and the most coveted laminate badges on Earth. A guy carrying a guitar case bumped into me and rushed off without saying sorry. We were shown to a room with tables and folding chairs, vases of flowers and tons of food and booze. It was the infamous green room. We'd made it!

"Here you go, miss," the security guy told Mary. "You can make yourself at home while you wait for Gary. If you want to watch the show, the stage is right down there," he told her, pointing down a long concrete tunnel.

Any hopes I had of waiting for Damien in the green room disappeared when the security guy pulled me into an empty dressing room and slammed the door behind us. He kissed me and started putting his hands all over me. He smelled like garlic and tasted like old cheese. I wanted to spew, but I reminded myself that it was all for Damien. He was all that mattered.

The security guy pushed me down on my knees and undid his fly as wild screams greeted In Dreams less than a hundred yards away. At least I could hear the music.

By the time I was shoved into the green room, the after-party was in full swing. The security guard thrust me through the door, smirking. He turned to go, then spun back to me.

"Oh," he said, "here."

He threw two laminates on the floor at my feet and walked away, laughing. I felt beyond scummy.

Until I looked around and saw the actual band mingling with other beautiful people!

I pulled my compact and lipstick out of my purse and did a little discreet touch up. I still looked hot despite my vigorous warm-up activities.

I walked to a table crowded with an assortment of liquor bottles and grabbed a bottle of beer, some imported kind. Wow. There was Scotty! He was so adorable. Dressed in jeans and a white T-shirt, he so lived up to his down-to-earth persona. He was amazing. He was also leaving. I drank my beer.

Standing alone in a sea of people, I heard an unmistakable voice crooning a verse from my favorite song.

My breath caught in my throat as I turned and saw him across the crowded room. It was totally like a dream. His blue eyes sparkled as he laughed with someone I couldn't see through the crowd. His dark hair was sweaty but perfect. And his smile... Oh, my God!

Then, my heart absolutely and completely broke.

Damien pulled a girl close to his side and dropped his hand onto her behind. I did not see her face, but I didn't have to. Her short black hair topped the familiar skinny-ass frame. Her bony shoulders shook as she laughed at Damien's corny jokes. That stupid dog collar was unmistakable. Damn it. That bitch whore. I wanted to scream. And cry. And break stuff.

Damien waved good-bye to everyone in the room. His sapphire eyes even met mine for a brief second, but by then, I was so beyond caring. He pulled bitch-whore out the door, and they were gone.

I chugged my beer and reached for another.

I know, right?

JOHN

Friday, July 7

It wasn't always like this, my street, my neighborhood. We didn't have poofy coffee houses or elite art galleries or posh hair salons. That stuff is all new. When I was little, we had convenience stores with sheets of plywood covering broken windows, abandoned industrial buildings, rusted-out tire-less cars perched on cement blocks and tagged with graffiti. Hookers, junkies, pimps, pushers, gang-bangers, and just plain poor weirdoes came out at dusk and shambled along the sidewalks, looking for love or money. It wasn't as dangerous as Compton or South Central on account of the big office buildings that were close by, but it was pretty shitty.

Then, one day, some hot-shot rich guy drove through on his way to LAX and had a 'vision.' He made some phone calls, talked to some high-profile people, and held a few meetings and press conferences. After that, a huge metamorphosis, sparked by the conversion of one grubby mom-and-pop convenience store to a bright and shining Starbucks, changed our lives forever. There was an evolutionary explosion.

Mexican day-laborers started showing up, crammed into rusted-out pick-up trucks, blasting their obnoxious horn-heavy music. Bigger trucks loaded with sheets of drywall and panes of glass followed, everyone yelling in Spanish, talking to each other in loud, excited exclamations. The whole scene was like a Brownsville family reunion at the hardware store.

I'd shut my window and plug in my iPod, desperate to escape the dust, the jackhammers and the cackling of a hundred real-life Speedy Gonzaleses. You'd think it would have quieted down at night, to give us a rest. But, no, the developers must have been some greedy bastards because those noisy fucks gutted buildings around the clock for weeks. I couldn't study (not that I ever really tried), I couldn't sleep, I couldn't paint, I couldn't even read my goddamn Black Jack comic books. All I could do was plug my ears with Minor Threat while I nodded out, high on heroin, and scratch still-lifes in my sketchbook.

Mom didn't seem too stressed by the commotion. Of course, she was usually at work. Or drunk. The only thing that bugged her was the prospect of our landlord trying to kick us out in favor of some higher-paying tenants, now that he suddenly owned property in one of the hippest neighborhoods in the city. It seemed likely that he'd pull some shit like that. I mean, I would if I owned the place. But, so far, he was either too nice or too stupid to raise the rent or kick us out. Mom, in her rare lucid moments, said it was just a matter of time before we would be out on the street.

Near the end of the construction phase, the synthetic real estate people showed up in their Volvo SUVs to post 'for sale' signs in the new floor-to-ceiling windows of the renovated 'artist lofts.' Sometimes they'd have the balls to shoo me away from my perch on the steps, but mostly they'd just ignore me. To them, I was just another germ-ridden indigenous pest. Maybe they should have tried shining a light on me to see if I'd scurry into the sewer or something.

Soon, the trend-setting hipsters descended. All silicone implants, perfect hair, and blindingly white teeth framed by Botox perma-smiles. Assholes. They abandoned their Beverly Hills estates in droves, desperate to gain more 'street cred' by 'keeping it real' and moving downtown. The whole thing made me want to puke. Fucking idiots, couldn't leave us poor folks alone. They didn't have the brains to realize they were driving up the rent prices and forcing my neighbors into the street.

However, I do have to admit, the infusion of Hollywood cash was a boon to my own personal economy. Those young creative types definitely loved to party. No longer was my income limited to nickel and dime pot sales to my perpetually broke classmates; I made a hill of coin supplying stuff to a handful of my new rich neighbors. Bonus: those fiscally gifted casual users even tipped.

I didn't make *that* much dough, though. I was still a poor ghetto kid, but after they showed up, I could at least order off of something other than the dollar menu and buy new Docs. My mom and I lived in a dirty cramped two-bedroom apartment in one of the old buildings. Mom wasn't home much, like I said, working two jobs, and she was drunk when she was there. She'd leave me a couple of bucks for food every few days, whenever she could, but by the time I was thirteen, I didn't need her money. I squirreled away what little she gave me in an old peanut butter jar under my bed. Then I'd sneak it, little by little, back into her purse while she was passed out. I used to think about saving it up to buy myself a car, but I didn't really have anywhere to go. I was pretty much stuck there. At least until someone decided to shoot me or stab me to death in some dark alley.

In the fading sun of early evening, I'd set up shop on the steps of the renovated apartment building across the street from my own. It was summer, but my classmates dropped by once in a while to make small purchases. I wasn't well-liked at school, but I was well-known, mostly for being the punk creep who won all the art shows. I was a freak, a loser.

"Hey, John, dude, what's up?" A pock-faced kid strolled up, shadowed by two of his grubby-looking friends. They were looking for some action.

"Hey, man. Just hangin,'" I said.

Two of the guys were shop monkeys at school, typical gearheads. I couldn't think of their names, but I knew their faces. They wanted a little weed, couple of hits of X, acid, whatever I had that week. Money changed hands. Product followed.

"This shit better be real, dog," said Pock-Marks, sniffing a joint, squinting at a pill.

One of the other guys looked like he was tripping already, swaying in a vaguely circular motion, muttering to himself.

"Guaranteed. Dude, what's with your friend?" I asked, jerking a thumb toward the swaying kid, shuffling bills in my hands.

"That's his brother," Pock-Marks said, pointing to the other guy I recognized from school. "Check this, yo — dude thinks he's a fucking pitcher of orange juice. Right now, see what he's doing? That swirling shit?" Pock-Marks mimicked a hula. "He's 'stirring his concentrate.' Watch."

Pock-Marks reached out and gave the Swaying Kid a push. It wasn't a hard shove, but to Swaying Kid, it was like pushing the plunger on an explosive device strapped to his chest. The nudge totally and violently ripped him from his fruit-filled fantasy world.

"Oh, my God! Fuck!"

Swaying Kid's eyes flew wide open, his arms shot out in an effort to steady himself. His pupils were enormous.

"Do not fucking spill me! I told you not to touch me, man!"

He reminded me of Crispin Glover in that old *River's Edge* movie, screaming about Feck.

"If I spill my goddamn juice, I'm dead. I will be empty! You know what that means, man? Gone! Fucked!"

I had seen some strange shit, but this was completely insane. Most of my customers were just casual users, like me. I didn't carry enough product to satisfy the hardcore junkies. They only came to me in a pinch, when no one else was holding. And, to tell you the truth, I was glad because those guys scared the shit out of me. I could see right where the Swaying Juice Kid was headed.

The rage melted from the Swaying Kid's face. He took on an air of resignation, fatigue.

"Do you know how much of my life just evaporates every day?" The anger returned, but at a lower volume. "Don't you ever fucking touch me again."

I stared in silence. The Swaying Kid had calmed down, retreated back into his carafe. I looked at Pock-Marks, who shot a glance at the kid's brother and busted out laughing.

"That's fucked up," I said. "What did he say? His life evaporates? Why doesn't he get a lid, you know, like a hat or something?"

Lame. I didn't know what else to say. It was kind of funny, but it made me a little sick, too. It reminded me of the first time a total coke fiend came to me for a quick fix. The guy, shaking, sweating, and in a total panic, whispered sweet nothings to a brown half-eaten banana that he carried like a pet, as if it was the one wigging out. It was totally surreal. I swore I'd never be like that. I was only eleven when I started using, but I instinctively knew where that line was between use and abuse, and I saw how freaking bad it was to cross it.

I swallowed hard and looked down at the wad of cash in my clammy fist as the gearheads took off. I wished I could find a new job.

"Hey, John, man, what's up?"

A lanky guy, with what they call 'movie star good looks,' bounded out of the door behind me and plopped down almost in my lap. Personal space was a foreign concept to that dude. He gripped a black Stratocaster and a green bottle of San Pellegrino, two objects he kept close at all times.

This was the one and only Jeff Cole, aka Damien Tungsten. In case you've been in a coma for the last four years and don't know, he was the original lead heart-throb in the smash boy band, In Dreams. Can I get an 'oooooooh'?

Damien had moved into the building across the street

from mine about a year before. He was one of those new in-search-of-street-cred immigrants from the Hollywood Hills. That guy had it all, man: money, chicks, fame, money, looks, chicks... I thought life was so unfair and random. I hated that prick. But, for a boy band faggot, I guess he wasn't so bad. Then.

When he first moved in, this girl on the street started freaking out when she saw him. I thought he was going to be a real prima donna pain-in-the-ass and go into asshole mode. But he was super nice to her, which was a total shock. I'd seen those young actors and musicians around town, and they always acted like total asswipes, especially when some tourist would have the balls to tiptoe up to them and dare to ask for an autograph. But Damien's nice guy act was a total sham, which I, personally fell for after he'd been around for a couple of months.

I never thought Damien Tungsten would hang with a loser like me, but we used to get along okay. I mean, I still hated the dude because he was in a boy band, and I resented the hell out of the fact that he probably only hung with me out of pity, but what the hell, at least I had someone to talk to. He was only a few years older than me, and he had some unbelievably fantastic road stories. He was twenty-one, and he had the world by the short hairs. Gotta respect that. So he got a manicure every week and wore make-up — who didn't?

"Hey, douche bag, you need another lesson?"

I grabbed the Strat from him and plucked a couple of strings. I was not on a name-calling basis with anyone else, mind you. I was a total loner, super shy, and just really into my own shitty world. But, Damien used to have this way about him that just, I don't know, put me at ease. Does that sound stupid? Well, I guess it was.

I did have one thing going for me: I was a way better guitarist than my pal Damien. Just to emphasize that point, I cranked out a riff from 'How Soon is Now.' It was only three chords, but still, Johnny Marr would have been damn proud. And Damien was impressed. A jealous smirk painted his face, but he was humbled. Mission accomplished.

"Shit, *I* should be in a fucking boy band."

That always made him laugh. I knew he thought I was just a punk-ass kid, but tons of fifteen-year-olds signed mega record deals, headlined money making tours, starred in their own shows on the Disney Channel. He had done it. Too bad I couldn't get in on that kind of deal, I thought. I could sing alright in the shower, but there was no freaking way I would ever try that shit in front of an audience.

I had no illusions about the way my life was laid out. I was a poor downtown kid with shitty grades in a shitty school. Education wasn't my thing. And my social life... I didn't have any friends. Girls were unattainable. To them, I was invisible. Average-looking guys in Los Angeles, by the way, don't score. All the girls want Justin Bieber or... Damien Tungsten. And I was pretty freaking far from either one of them. I was rail-thin and nondescript, typical punk wannabe, complete with Black Flag tattoo and stud through my bottom lip. I wasn't hideous or anything. Just painfully transparent.

Damien always had girls over at his place, after shows and stuff. He'd offered to set me up a couple of times, but I was just way too shy. And getting me a date was always offered conditionally — I'd have to go to one of his shows and bring some of my product. Since I didn't want to actually bear witness to one of his embarrassing performances, I declined with a laugh and a caustic 'no fucking way.' I would have been the only guy in the audience. Which might not sound bad, but when every girl in the place is totally focused on my neighbor, I would have felt a little inferior, know what I mean?

Christ, I'd make a fool out of myself trying to talk to a girl. Even the nerd girls at school. I settled for admiring them from afar. The best thing about the influx of the hottie hipsters, aside from their tipping, few of them had window coverings. Voyeurism became my new hobby. Best seventy bucks I ever spent was on that Astro/Terrestrial telescope. And Damien, unwittingly, of course, had provided me with many evenings of late-night entertainment.

"You working on any cool drawings or anything, kid?" Damien asked, taking a sip of his mineral water, eyes rolling upward to follow a passing traffic helicopter.

He pushed me toward visual art, I think, because of my superior guitar playing. Heh.

I loved art, but I knew that it took a hell of a lot of lucky breaks to make it in that business — just like any kind of show biz. And I had no luck at all. I was certain that I'd wind up dead of an overdose or some other act of violence by age twenty-three. My only hope was that my undiscovered art would become famous after my tragic death.

I was a realist even at fifteen.

"I got a couple of projects going," I said, plucking a guitar string, *ping*.

His guitar was always out of tune. I don't think he even knew it. He was more about looks than technicalities.

I hadn't always been a loner. I did have a friend once, a kid from the apartment building next door. His name was Hank Jessup. He was a year older than me and was really into punk music. I was eleven years old when we started huffing glue in his bedroom. I have him to thank for my introduction to two things: getting high and punk rock.

"Hey," I told Damien, "listen to this."

I plucked out a simplified version of an old song by The Fall, which I was sure he'd never heard. He thought The Fall was just a season. Retard. The song had been Hank's favorite. I felt my eyes get moist as I strummed.

One day, I came home from school to find an ambulance parked in front of Hank's building. When I got to my apartment, his mom was there with her head buried in my mom's shoulder, sobbing and saying his name. Hank had been huffing furniture polish on the roof. I would have been with him if I hadn't gotten detention for smoking in the bathroom. I always felt a little guilty about not being there with him. His mom moved away the next week. I still miss that kid sometimes.

Getting high was fun, but it was nothing to die over. I could get along without drugs if I had to, as long as I had my art. Yeah, drugs were a lot easier to use than a paintbrush, but they could really mess you up if you weren't careful. Besides, I got a bigger rush off of showing other people what had started as an image inside my own head.

I had a mentor in my neighborhood, too.

It was not boy band grand master Damien.

It was the filthy bum who walked towards us, lugging what looked like a rusty old transmission case. That was infinitely cooler than the cheap Mexican Stratocaster that hung from my fist. I thrust the guitar at Damien and stood up.

"Patrick," I yelled. "How are you, man? How about smoking a bowl with us? I was just teaching Damien some new chords."

DAMIEN

Friday, July 7

Little shit. Yeah, he should be in a boy band alright. Ha. Kid has no fucking clue what it takes to make it in the business. All the six a.m. morning show radio interviews; driving across the country in a fucking bus that smells like weed, shit, and loneliness; not being able to walk into a 7-11 for a Big Gulp without getting mobbed. Fucker thinks he can play guitar better than me. Yeah, right. In his dreams. I don't know what he sees in that fucked up art fag, but better that he wants to follow in that fuck-up's footsteps. Last thing I need is more competition.

I totally love this neighborhood, though, and hanging with this arrogant little fuck. I don't know where he gets it, but I'll buy the occasional toot of coke off the kid and I'll be high for two days. Great stuff. I'll get something from him before I leave for the gig. We're playing the Palladium tonight — I am so psyched. It's gonna be a fucking great show. Hometown crowd, full house, all our local crew. Sweet. I'm guessing lots of perky Hollywood pussy, too. Ah, I love L.A.

I gotta go get dressed. Why can't they send a fucking hair and make-up bitch over to me? Christ.

JOHN

Friday, July 7

Patrick Salinger.

I was convinced that dude was destined to be the next Andy Warhol or Shepherd Fairey. He did some fantastically sick shit. He used to do these incredible pop art silkscreens that would put those big guys to shame. The first time I went to his loft, I almost had a stroke because of this enormous three-panel canvas — his first triptych — hanging on one of the towering concrete walls in what was his living room area.

Each ten-by-ten foot canvas featured the same image: a Frankenstein-type face all stitched together from parts that didn't quite match. The sheer scale of those things alone was enough to knock me on my ass, but, man, they were mad creepy, too. They were Warhol-esque, each one on a different colored background, but there was something kind of, I don't know, *otherworldly* about them. You couldn't tell from far away, but the stitches that held the facial parts together weren't painted on; they were actual black suture wire sewn into the canvas. That freaked me out. Also, parts of the skin had been peeled away, and there were patches of raw, slick, striated meat showing through. I was never really sure how he made it look so real or what materials he'd used. The 'skin' even looked real. Those things creeped me out, man. I could not imagine having those gigantic mutilated faces looming over me while I was watching TV or trying to sleep or eat or whatever. You have any idea what those things are worth today, though? Outrageous.

Lately, though, Patrick had gotten into making these really heavy installation pieces. Something like David Lynch used to do, with rotting meat, you know? Or that British guy who banked his own blood and then froze it in a self-portrait bust thing? Patrick had been doing a lot of Dumpster diving and using whatever junk he fished out. He was on the verge of a humungous breakthrough.

No one could have guessed just how huge.

Anyway, he declined my offer to socialize with me and Damien on that fateful evening. When I asked him if he wanted a toke, he brushed by me with a smirk and disappeared into the apartment building he shared with the King of Boy Bandland. Typical. He wouldn't talk to anyone when he was in 'the zone.' Also, he'd just been through a hellacious breakup with his girlfriend and probably needed some space.

"Well, okay, catch you later, then," I said to the closing door. I grabbed Damien's mineral water and took a swig, paying no attention to his grimace. "That dude's awesome. He's going to be the next Picasso or some shit."

As I said that, something poked at my brain like a dull thorn from a dead rose. I pictured Patrick's gaunt pale face leering at me, his platinum bangs covering one steely gray eye. I shuddered.

"Or the next Jeffrey Dahmer, maybe. He's kind of spooky. You know what I mean?"

Damien laughed, but I was serious. I wasn't scared of much, but there was just something not right about that guy.

Rumors swirled around the neighborhood about Patrick. Most of the talk revolved around his garbage wrangling and how disgusting that was. Like I said, he used mostly found objects, and he was known to mix in a fair amount of road kill. And people — whether they're from Compton or Bel Air — are all creeped out by a guy who digs through trash and plays with rotting animal carcasses.

Kids also love a good horror story, of course, and Patrick made an outstanding local version of the boogey man, especially with his creepy wraith-like appearance.

One night, I was sitting in the alley, listening to a couple of the little kids talk shit. One story that came out involved Patrick killing a coyote with his bare hands in a fight over a half-eaten candy bar. Luis Garcia, who had been a fourth grader at the time, loved to tell that story, man. His voice dropped to little more than a whisper, his eyes got real big, and he looked around to make sure no grown-ups were around. That kid was little, but he could tell one scary-ass story.

"Once upon a time, on a hot moonlit night," Luis began with his usual dramatic flair, "Patrick Salinger stood in the darkest back alley in all of downtown, right behind my papi's taco stand, over there."

He lifted a finger toward a tiny fluorescent-lit plywood lunch counter across the street. Garcia's Taco Stand, 'Best Churros in L.A.,' according to the hand-painted sign.

"Dude stood hip deep in half-eaten moldy burritos and rotten avocados, clawing through grease soaked pizza boxes and plastic bags filled with dog shit."

Little Jimmy Torres studied Luis's face with wide-eyed anticipation. I wore a bored *yeah, whatever* expression, but — even though I'd heard the story before, from several sources — I was just as transfixed. For me, the story was an unwelcome herald of things much more horrible to come.

"Underneath a wet *L.A. Weekly* with salsa smeared across the torn front page," Luis continued, "his hand closed around something squishy but chunky. The thing was half-wrapped in a piece of crinkly plastic." Luis scanned each of our faces. "It was a Baby Ruth."

"Oooh, scary, Luis," said David Fillmore.

He was a smart-ass twelve-year-old whose mom was a hooker.

"Hey, I laid a Tootsie Roll in my toilet this morning that would have you screaming your head off."

"Shut up, dickhead," little Jimmy shot back, sticking out his tongue and grabbing his crotch for emphasis.

"Hot breath on the back of Patrick's neck and a soft rumbling sound told him that he wasn't alone," said Luis, unfazed by the David/Jimmy exchange. "He slowly turned around. Right behind him, crouching on top of a big pile of garbage, was the biggest damn coyote west of Riverside. The thing's yellow eyes squinted, its tail lowered, its mouth widened, and Patrick sprang."

Luis jumped up, shooting his right hand out in a cobra strike. Jimmy and David also jumped.

"His hand shot forward faster than Jackie Chan, and he choked the life out of that mean thing."

We all looked at each other as police sirens whined in the near distance.

"After that," Luis finished, "he dragged the body home and taught himself how to do taxidermy. He uses the stuffed coyote as a footstool," he said, looking at David. "No one knows what happened to the Baby Ruth — maybe it's in your mama's underwear."

Or so the story went. The gospel according to Luis. Thanks be to Garcia. That kid had a story about everybody. There were others about Patrick, but, for reasons that will become obvious, that is the one I remember most clearly.

I wonder if Luis ever told any stories about me after everything was all over. I'll bet he did.

Anyway, the few times I'd been in Patrick's apartment, I'd never seen a coyote, stuffed or otherwise. And despite all the rumors and ghost stories, he had seemed like a pretty okay guy to me. Just an artist. What I wanted to be when I grew up. Artists were supposed to be a little... different.

Well, okay, he scared the piss out of me. I guess it was the stories, or... I don't even know. He just gave me a bizarre vibe, that's all. It was like being around something you know looks scary, but can make you look cool by association, you know? Like, maybe, driving a hearse, or being friends with a gang-banger. You know people look at you, thinking you must have balls, but inside you're going, *"Yo, this shit's kind of tripping me out."*

Whatever.

Patrick was a scary kind of cool.

That night, hours before I saw Damien commit murder, the sun crashed down somewhere in Santa Monica. I was feeling pleasantly mellow, just hanging out on the steps of Patrick's building, sketching my bedroom window from the exterior. Who should come stomping out the door behind me but my idol, the boogeyman himself, Mr. Patrick Salinger. In my mind's bloodshot eye, he was wearing a black turtleneck and a beret. I stifled a laugh, but apparently, not well.

"Hey, John. What's so funny? Dude, you smell like an Amsterdam coffeehouse."

He wore black eyeliner and looked somehow skeletal. He looked like one of those old- school skater types you see everywhere. He wore eyeliner, like Billy Joe Armstrong, some lame checkerboard Vans, and seriously outdated oversized flannel. I didn't go for that, but, whatever. I wasn't going to tell him that he looked like a pussy. My picture would wind up on a milk carton or some shit.

"Doing some drawing, huh?"

That dude had a wicked grasp of the obvious.

"Yeah, wanna see?"

I held out my sketchbook.

He took it in his cut-up bony hand and studied it for about thirty seconds (or ten years, if you were in my neighborhood of mellowosity). I wondered if he was awestruck by my super-skilled technical architectural rendering of the rotting dentil molding, or if the scary little demon with the coyote eyes dripping down the bricks spoke to him.

"That's very interesting." He handed the book back. "Keep up the good work, dude."

He clapped me on the shoulder a little too hard. It sent a chill down the back of my neck.

"Hey, I got some really choice chronic from upstate this

morning," I said, shivering. "Wanna buy some? I'll cut you a sweet deal if you let me see what you're working on."

I loved that guy's art, man. Did I say that already? I don't think I could say it enough. I was always trying to get a peek, but success was a rare treat. Patrick was pretty private, kept to himself — which everyone would say in the papers, ad nauseam, that Fall.

He chuckled, flashing a dazzling crescent moon grin that sparkled through the dusk.

"John, John, John... Sorry, pal, but I'm totally tapped at the moment."

He shook out a cigarette and felt around for his lighter.

"Hey, why haven't you been going to school the last few days?"

"Summer vacation," I said, lighting him up. "Too bad you're tapped, man. This is some good shit. I got so fucked up the other night I ate raw liver because I thought it would make me fly."

I couldn't help laughing a little at the hazy memory. I mean, I knew it wasn't funny, and I know that "this is your brain on drugs" and all that, but, you know, I had to have fun sometimes. Life was hard; I owned a helmet.

"Hey, you should have seen that chick in the building next door to you last night. She was sucking this guy so hard..."

Patrick gave me a sideways look through the curtain of his bangs, turning to leave.

"You know, I'm so glad I have curtains on my windows, living across the street from a little acid-head perv like you."

But he said it pretty good-natured, you know, not like he thought I was really evil or anything.

"Hey, man, I'm an artist, too. I just don't have the cash to take anatomy or life drawing classes or whatever." I smiled.

He rolled his eyes and took off, shaking his head and shooting me a backward wave.

The rest of that early evening was pretty uneventful. The calm before the storm, as they say, right? Oooh. Shit.

I smoked a couple of joints, sold a couple more, and worked on my drawing.

An hour or three later, I was seriously hating life.

JOHN

Friday, July 7 — Saturday, July 8

I was still sitting on Patrick/Damien's steps when the limo pulled up. The back door flung open, and Damien's highly coveted Diesel jean clad ass emerged, followed by his black suede Adidas Campus shoes. He'd played a show at the Palladium and was just getting home with what appeared to be a groupie firmly attached to his lips.

The kiss broke with an audible pop as she climbed out of the car. Skinny goth knockout, jet black hair, knobby knees and black lips, bright, wondering, eyes riveted to Damien's. She wore this really slutty black lacy tank top thing (maybe some kind of underwear?) and the microest skirt I'd ever seen. To complete the look, she sported fourteen-inch screaming red heels, and — ho ho ho — a black leather dog collar, complete with tag. She looked pretty young, though, even for Damien. He slammed the car door, and they giggled past me.

Hmm, I had to get in on that.

I snapped my sketch book shut, gathered up my pencils and shit, and took off across the street. I tripped as I ran up the threadbare piss-stained staircase to my place on the third floor. Mom was nodding off in front of our old Flintstones TV with her latest lover, Jack Daniels, a cigarette burning dangerously close to her withered fingers. Pity, shame, alarm, and hopelessness all colored my vision. I hated seeing her that way. I absolutely fucking hated that scene. I crossed the cramped room, squeezed around the battered coffee table and took the cigarette from her small hand. As I ground the butt out in an ashtray swiped from the Frolic Room, Mom cracked her eyes open.

"Sweetheart. Is it time for bed already?"

The slur in her voice and the rotten dead smell that rose with her words made my skin crawl and my heart ache. My stomach turned, and I felt like crying. Sometimes — a lot of the time, actually — I was more like the parent in our broken household. I resented it, but it was the role I was destined to play.

"Yeah, Ma. It's pretty late. You should go to bed."

She'd probably sleep on the couch. She didn't spend many nights in her sway-back double bed. Maybe she thought it wasn't worth the effort to walk ten feet down the hall to the bed that my father hadn't been in for nine years. Maybe she was just too tired or drunk, I didn't know, but she spent a lot of nights on the sofa.

"Okay, honey," she said to me, and then her eyes slipped shut.

She was thirty-five, but she looked at least sixty. She was pretty once, my mom. Greta Thomas, nee Johnston. She met my dad in Milwaukee about two years before I was born. She had just graduated from high school and had taken a receptionist job at some real estate office.

My father, who had delivered those big water cooler jugs, came in on her first day and asked her out. They dated for a few months, then mom got pregnant. My father, Mr. Tom Thomas, had been planning a big move to Hollywood, where he was convinced he'd be the next Tom Cruise or Harrison Ford or some ridiculous damn thing. Mom never told me straight out, but I think he was disappointed that he'd had a wife and kid tying him down. She'd agreed to move west with him, where they would get married, get jobs, and raise me. Well, they did get married, they did get jobs, and she raised me.

Turned out that my father had the looks but not the ability to memorize lines, so he worked a couple of modeling jobs. Print ads, not TV or anything, mostly clothing — suits, trench coats, conservative stuff. He blamed Mom for his 'failure,' and they both started drinking. Eventually, he took off and left me and Mom on our own. I don't know what happened to him. He must be dead since he never came looking for me, even after all the media hype.

Anyway, Mom got a job in some plastics factory here, during the day, and she cleaned offices at night. I went to daycare after school up until I was about eight, and then she just couldn't afford it anymore, so I'd taken care of myself ever since. And, yeah, I kind of take care of her, too. I tried not to blame her too much for the way things had turned out.

After draping a holey fleece blanket over her, I turned to go down the hall to my own room. On my way, I had to squeeze past our little plastic kitchen table. A pile of bills sat next to Mom's dirty purse. I looked over my shoulder to make sure she wasn't watching, then I took the wad of bills I had in my pocket, peeled off a twenty for myself, and put the rest in her handbag.

Okay, okay, nothing to see here, virtuous son bit over.

It was show time.

I stepped into my room and locked the door behind me, pulling off my shirt with one hand. My room smelled like dirty socks, smoke, ammonia, and B.O. There was no getting used to it. I nearly gagged every time I walked in. It didn't motivate me to clean up or anything, though. I stepped over a pile of dirty clothes and a stack of art books and assumed my place at the window.

I pulled out the tripod legs, locked them into place, and aimed my scope as quickly as I could, my movements accelerated by my growing excitement.

I saw Damien and the girl in his living room, kissing, touching. His hands, first on her shoulders, slithered down to her waist, and then settled on her breasts. She told him something with a seductive smile, laughed, and stroked his cheek. He kissed her, picked her up, and headed for the bedroom.

He held her as they seemed to devour each other's face. He pushed her down on the bed and took off his shirt. Above the window frame, I could see the top of her head, the tips of her now bare breasts, and her splayed knees with Damien standing naked in between them. My breathing grew heavier. They stayed that way for a minute or two, while I played along at home. Then they switched positions. He lay prone on the bed with her straddling him, naked except for the dog collar.

And that's when you came in. He choked her to death, then rolled her up in an oriental rug, and dragged her out of the building.

Back to me being in shock, hiding in my room, practicing some heavy-duty self-medication.

I had slunk back over to the window on my hands and knees and peeked out. Damien and his rug were gone. A silver limo idled on the street in front of Damien's building.

I lifted my eyes and found Damien in his third floor bedroom, grabbing clothes from his closet and throwing them on the bed. He was crying into the phone, pulling on his hair, pounding his fist on his chest. I felt like I should be sad, but that circuit was temporarily disconnected.

Damien put down the phone, did something to something on the bed, and walked through his apartment with a duffel bag. He opened his front door and walked out. Seconds later, he burst through the building's double front doors and stood stock still at the top of the steps. Some inexplicable magnetic force pulled his face skyward.

His eyes locked right onto my own.

Flash.

I trembled in my window as he leapt into the waiting car and took off.

Holy shit, Batman.

I sat there, trapped in my own private Hitchcock movie.

I wished like hell that Ashton Kutcher would show his fugly baby-face and tell me that I had just been most heinously and viciously Punk'd.

JOHN

Saturday, July 8

Decades oozed by as I lay shivering in a pool of cold sweat. The sounds of my mother clanking around in the kitchen told me that it was 4:30 a.m. My insides churned as I fought to contain the riot of noise that raged in my head.

Damien Tungsten killed someone.

And he saw me.

He saw me see him commit murder and then flee the scene. ?!?!

No. It couldn't be real. My brain refused to accept that shit. Just... no. Damien existed in the same invincible bubble of purity we bestow upon all celebrities who reach a certain level of status. He could not commit murder. Absolutely not true. No fucking way.

But yes, the murder was real. It was as real as Barack Obama. It was as real as that old *Kung Fu/Kill Bill* dude hanging himself in a closet. It was as real as the hangnail on my left thumb.

I wanted to puke. I wanted to crawl into a hole and hide for a hundred years. I wanted to shoot heroin until I reached an irreversible level of unconsciousness. I wanted a drink of water.

I reached for my ancient Coke and sent a jar of paintbrushes crashing to the floor. Footsteps thumped in the short hallway outside my hellish cell. Mom tapped on my balsa wood door.

"John, are you okay in there?" She rattled the locked door knob.

"Yeah, Mom, I'm okay," I croaked, even though I was pretty freaking far from okay. "I... I just dropped my brushes." I couldn't pick them up; I was frozen.

"You're up awfully early today. Must be working on something good, huh?"

She was shouting from the kitchen. I had been known, on occasion, to become totally engrossed in my painting or drawing and pull an unintentional all-nighter.

I didn't say anything. I wanted to, but nothing came out. I wanted to tell my Mommy about the bad man across the street. I wanted to cry like a baby and hide behind her, where I'd be safe from all evil. I needed the comfort I'd never known, even when I was small.

"You'd better not be smoking that stuff again, John. I thought I smelled it in the hall there." She inhaled deeply, paused, exhaled. Smoking. "I gotta get to work. Then, I have to go out to the Valley and help Grandma. She's real sick again, you know." I heard her coffee cup *thud* on the bottom of the stainless steel sink. "You call me if you need anything. Love you, kiddo."

"Love you, too, Mom," I croaked.

I didn't know when I'd see her again. I wanted to hug her, to let her hug me, wrap me in her arms and hide my eyes. Instead, I stared blindly at a spider web in the corner above my desk and shook like a broken washing machine.

I heard the front door open and close, the deadbolt click. My breath leaked out like air from a pinhole in an old balloon. I crawled to the window and watched Mom walk down our front steps, down the block and disappear around the corner. Rows of dark windows and pinkish streetlights glinted from the silent pre-dawn wasteland.

Something stirred on the periphery.

My focus was once again drawn to a figure on the flight of steps across the street.

This one *ascending*, rather than *descending*.

This one did not lug a rolled up Oriental rug *down*, but rather hauled it *up*.

No. It couldn't be.

I ducked below my window frame, grazing my brow on the way down. Panic squeezed my throat to a pinhole and twisted my intestines. Someone was screaming inside my splitting skull. I think it was me.

I had to look again.

Patrick.

Oh. My. God. I couldn't breathe. I banged my head against the wall over and over, like I did as a toddler, trying to erase the image. What the fuck was he doing?

The revelation hit me like a Mack truck.

Early morning Dumpster diving.

He found it.

He found *her*.

The coyote project on a grander scale.
Flash.

PATRICK

Thursday, November 2

Dear John,

I want you to know that I cried when I found her. Let's get that straight right now. Everyone was so goddamned obsessed with my 'absolute lack of empathy.' Give me a break. No one knew what I thought, what I felt. No one had the balls to even hint at the possibility that I may have mourned her.

I saw that rug jammed into a corner of that big dumpster next to your building. My initial thought was *Hey, that might look good in my apartment.* I scaled the box's low blue wall and jumped in, landing on a heap of lumpy white kitchen bin liners and plastic grocery store bags, all stuffed with the residue of everyday living. The rug's color pattern seemed vaguely familiar, but, damn my memory, I would never place it, even though I'd walked on it a dozen times or more.

I picked my way over to that corner and pulled the top of the roll toward me. It was heavier than I'd expected, and I had to work to find a better foothold between the cocoons of rubbish. When I was finally able to see into the cylinder, there was something black and kind of stringy about a foot and a half down. I yanked at the carpet and recognized the top of a head. My heartbeat quickened, my mouth watered. I whipped my head around to make sure that I was alone in the alley. The mouth of an open can bit my ass as I sat down hard. What to do, what to do.

There was a *body* rolled up in that rug. No, not just a body, but a *person*. The second my mind wrenched that particular word from the clamoring panic in my head, tears spilled from my eyes. So, yeah, there you go, I cried. And that wasn't the only time, either. But you know that.

Tears of sorrow or tears of joy? I can't really say. I can tell you that I had pawed through the trash cans and Dumpsters in that neighborhood for almost a solid year, looking for the single object that would propel me to artistic legend. I killed a dog once — *not* a coyote like some of the kids think, and it was probably someone's pet — and I enjoyed some minor success from reworking its well-fed frame. You didn't know that, did you? I never told you because I thought it might upset you. Kind of like the girl. Anyway, this... This was different.

This was the Opportunity of a Lifetime.

I had never been what you'd call an over-achiever. In fact, I had always been extremely average, a totally vanilla suburbanite with totally typical skills and abilities. And, then, like you, sometime around eighth grade, I found art. I mean, I could never paint or draw that well, but I did other stuff. I could take someone else's product and give it an entirely new meaning. I could make it special. And it, in turn, could make me special. Bizarre objects yield loads of attention — remember that, kid.

I was about thirteen when I put together my first installation piece. It consisted of a small table, a half-exploded bean bag chair, and a live hamster in one of those plastic exercise ball things. I had to talk my art teacher into letting me set it up at the school art fair. I didn't win a ribbon or anything, but I did catch the attention of a local art professor who had a kid at my school. He told my mother that she should enroll me in some classes at the Brentwood Art Center, which she did happily enough, even though it was hell to get there after school and it made my dad crazy.

Dad wanted me to play football and be on the debate team, the regular junior Captain of Industry type. I embarked upon a creative rebellion, and I absolutely relished it, but... I don't know. Part of me always felt like a failure. That's what started me on this mad quest for fame and acceptance.

I had a couple of successful shows a few years ago, as you used to remind me, but I was still waiting for that mythical big break. My ex-girlfriend, who had been my biggest supporter since art school, gave me the big kiss-off last month because of my 'lack of success.' You remember — we got so wasted that night, you and I, out on the steps. Anyway, I don't remember what I told you, but all her friends were getting married and having families, and she wanted to do the same. She was thirty-two, and her clock was ticking and blah, blah, blah.

"Patrick," she said, "you know I love you, and I think your work is good, but..."

She couldn't even look me in the eye; she looked at the floor.

"You haven't been too lucky lately." She came over and put her arms around my neck then, like she was going to be nice and everything. "Do you think that maybe it's time to settle down?"

I pushed her away, knowing what she was about to say. She wanted me to get a 'real job,' said graphic design or something like that would allow me to actually sell my 'art.' Well, logos and letterhead designs are *not* art. That's just pimping out your talent for a couple of bucks, squandering a God-given gift. But she just doesn't get that. And you'd do well to remember it yourself, buddy. Don't sell out, man. You've got talent.

Anyway, that was the first and the last time that I'd ever raised a hand to her. That bitch, telling me that I don't have what it takes. Fucking accountant, telling me what art is. Shit. It wasn't like she was paying my bills or rent — I had a fucking trust fund for that. She was tired of my 'professional failure.'

And I was tired of her telling me I wasn't good enough.

Just like my father. So, I smacked her across the face and told her to get the fuck out. And, as you know, she did.

And, so, that morning in the Dumpster, my chance at the big time had finally arrived. I'd show her. I'd show *him*. I'd show them all. I was going to make Damien Hirst look like a community college amateur.

Do you understand what I was getting at, John? I think you do. Thanks for helping me, anyway. The exhibition went well, don't you think? Ha. I can't believe everything got so fucked up.

Hey, I wondered what happened to you, you know.
Until I saw you on TV.
Prick.

Your Friend,

Patrick

JOHN

Saturday, July 8

Oh, God, oh, shit, oh, fuck. What was I supposed to do? I pretty much had to call the cops. Didn't I? God, they'd lock me up. I've been dealing drugs for years, using them, manu-fucking-facturing them, for Christ's sake. Not to mention looking in people's windows, occasionally swiping candy bars from Achmed's convenience store down the street, and skipping school. They'd definitely lock my ass up.

And, oh, Damien.

And Patrick.

That's it. That's the end of all our lives. We are all totally and irrevocably fucked.

That's the kind of stuff that blew through my mostly-empty teenaged head as I squatted in my room, stupidly agonizing over my own petty crimes. God, I was such a douche. I should have called the cops right then and there. But, what can I say, I was a stupid kid.

I leaned to my left and puked into the crumpled graphite abortions in my cobalt blue wastepaper basket. My room spun, random objects popped out at me, like in a funhouse mirror: my sketchbook with the scraped red cover, a glass jar half-filled with clear liquid, the ancient gooseneck desk lamp with the burnt out bulb, an open case of Sudafed, ratty old black Converse sneaker. I hurled again, totally missing the trash can.

Patrick wrestled the rug through the door as I knelt watching, welded to my window frame. My mouth hung open, fat strings of spit and bile stretched from the down-turned corners, almost reaching the carpet. Patrick heaved the rug up on one end against the brick next to the door-frame and used his back to prop open the heavy door. He yanked at the top of the roll and it fell, head first, through the crack he'd made, scraping his arm on its way down. He jumped back and cursed, letting the cylinder crumple to the floor. It lay across the threshold, like a giant fringed burrito. Patrick took a quick look up and down the street, then stepped on top of the roll and slipped through the doorway.

I collapsed on the floor and stared through the ceiling with bulging eyes. My mind reeled, a panicked jumble of denial and self-preservation tore through like a hurricane. My reptilian midbrain took over, and I slithered back to the window.

Oh, my God, was he really jerking that carpet through the door? My mind rejected the surreal image, trying to banish it from any accessible memory even as the scene unfolded before my eyes. It had to be a dream.

Maybe he didn't know what was inside, I lied to myself. My head throbbed and threatened to explode.

I reached under the bed for my most serious gear. If ever there was a time in my life that I needed to cook up, it was then. I mean, even if you've never done drugs, watching your buddy drag a dead body into his house might give you a pretty good excuse to take that first trip.

I gripped the end of my jean belt in my teeth, holding it tight enough to keep my veins from sinking, at the same time choking off the scream that fought like hell to rip out of my throat. I sunk the cold spike with the irrational hope of erasing everything, not only my memory but the very actions of my friends as well. Blood flowered back into the barrel of the syringe and I forced it back into my circulatory system. Serenity flowed through me almost as soon as I pressed the plunger.

I bobbed and floated on a sea of blissful oblivion. There

was no pain, only music and nothingness. David Bowie's 'Space Oddity' echoed through the blankness. *The stars look very different today.*

The phone. Was it ringing? Maybe. No. Who was I going to call? Yesss, the police. Something about Patrick. He made some beautiful stuff. Lovely, peaceful rust. Blissful images layered in trash. Something about a rug...

The rug.

Oh, no.

Oh, no. I fell through dense chilly fog. No, I didn't want to go back. Patrick. Patrick. Static in my head heralded the end of the calm. I suddenly remembered what drove me to that peaceful purgatory.

I had known that Hollywood had been moving into the 'hood, but this was way beyond theatrical. They had to be shooting some low-budget movie on my street. It couldn't be real. Damien wouldn't... Patrick wouldn't...

Tears dripped off my face, into my hands. I had no idea how long I sat there, crying. The dirty matted carpet beneath me was drenched when I finally struggled to my feet.

I had to go to the bathroom.

I floated across the hall and hovered over the toilet. I had to see Patrick. The thought thumped and swallowed me like a surfer's dream wave. I had to see what he was doing with it. *To* it.

With *her*, to *her*, I reminded myself.

I stooped over the sink, splashing cold water on my already freezing wet face. I *had* to do it. I *had* to go over there. I mean, he was my friend, wasn't he?

Of course I didn't want to. I didn't know what I thought I could do about the situation, but I wanted to see what was happening anyway. At that time, believe it or not, I did know the difference between right and wrong. I hoped my friend did, too. I mean, I thought he did.

I grabbed some clothes from my bedroom floor and pulled them on as I squeezed through the living room. I floated down the stairs and opened the big heavy door. Sunlight stabbed my eyes and, for a second, I thought I was going to puke again. Cars roared by in a steady stream, people chattered along the sidewalks, a helicopter thrummed overhead, a dog barked. Sensory overload.

I instinctively turned to go back to the darkened mess called home. If I could just lay in my bed and sleep, everything would be okay, I pleaded silently with moving lips.

What a fucking crock.

I knew damn well that I'd get into my bed, sweat buckets of something cold and sticky, and never be able to lie still. Sleep would not show me any mercy.

And nothing would be okay.

Nothing would ever be okay again.

I pushed myself down the steps and trudged across the street without looking both ways. A car honked as it blew by, my baggy T-shirt flapping in its wake. I sat down in my usual recreational spot on those damned steps for a second, thinking maybe Patrick would somehow sense my presence and come outside. *Yeah, sure, dickhead.* I knew that was supremely ridiculous, but, come on, I was seriously freaking out.

I crawled up to the double doors and heaved one open. It weighed four tons and took me the better part of seven months. An antiseptic scent of cleanliness wafted to my nostrils. The lobby's marble floor sparkled and gleamed, reflected back in each tiny diamond pendant that hung from the gaudy chandelier. The place was deserted. They were supposed to have a guard, but there was no one behind the desk. I crossed to the elevator and punched the up button twice. And I waited. Almost, but not quite, long enough to talk myself into running home like a coward.

I rode the elevator up to the floor that Patrick and Damien shared. I stepped out, my knees weak and rubbery. One drag on the cigarette I'd lit made me retch, so I dropped it on the marble floor and crushed it. Out of the corner of my eye, I regarded Patrick's artificially rusted steel door, wondering what he could possibly be doing in there. I glanced toward Damien's place with a surprising feeling of shame mixed with guilt. My feet carried me toward Apartment 4, totally ignoring my internal screams of protest. I raised my hand to knock on the door, also against my own will.

I lowered my fist without knocking — a small, if momentary, triumph of conscious self. I felt like crying. I drove my knuckles into my eyes, wiping away hot tears, damning myself for even being there.

I knocked.

Shuffling on the other side of the door. I imagined a gigantic cockroach scrabbling across curling linoleum. The peep hole darkened and then cleared. A forceful hiss, like a blast from the air compressor down at the gas station, sounded inside, making me jump. Then the door creaked open. A crack. I saw a slice of Patrick's gray eye.

"Yeah?" he said, not widening the crack. "What do you want, John?"

Fatigue tinged with impatience edged his voice.

In a move that surprised even me, I rushed the door, knocking Patrick backwards. I charged into the apartment and stood in the middle of Patrick's living space, gaping around the sparsely furnished concrete bunker. He slammed the front door and glared through me. I felt like puking and was proud of myself for holding it down.

"Where is she?" I demanded, trying to sound authoritative with my shiny new adolescent baritone.

"What? Who...? What...?"

Confusion. Feigned innocence. The fucker. At least he looked like he'd been crying. The air was thick with freshly sprayed aerosol roses.

"You know goddamn well who and what."

The ugly Frankenstein prints leered at me, mocking the cowardice that hid just below the surface of my skin.

Patrick's eyes darted across the cavernous room to the weathered steel bathroom door. I sprinted across the space,

Patrick on my heels, nearly tripping me.

"Don't! Let me..." he stammered, grabbing for my outstretched hand with both of his.

I threw open the bathroom door and fell inside. My shoulder and hip hit the concrete floor with a hollow pong. A smothering putrid stench hit me so hard I could taste it. I dry heaved in the general direction of the toilet.

"Let me explain," Patrick said, standing over me, mouth turned down, panic widening his eyes.

"You don't have to explain," I said, my eyes falling on the shape in the bathtub.

I gasped and gagged. I hurried to look away, hoping the thing wouldn't be there when I looked again. I could still see it out of the corner of my eye.

"I already know."

Patrick's eyes widened, and his mouth fell open, in some insufficient defensive argument, working like the lips of a dying fish. He looked profoundly scared.

Damien's date reclined in the tub. Her white skin had a bluish tinge that made me catch my breath. A crimson band of damaged flesh encircled her delicate neck. Her cloudy blue eyes pleaded with the exposed pipes and beams that supported the ceiling. Oh, my God, so, so awful. An invisible hand squeezed my heart.

"You already know what?" Patrick asked, regaining his composure.

I tore my watery eyes from the still figure and looked at him. How could he bring her here? What was he going to do? His uneasy face had hardened into a stoic mask of vacuity.

"Patrick." I could barely manage a whisper.

Coming here, confronting him, had been a huge mistake. One that I could not undo.

"I saw."

"What? What did you see?"

He shifted his weight, casually resting his hands on his hips, staring me down. He was challenging me, daring me.

"I saw you carry it in." I spat out the words like a wad of phlegm. "I saw you carry *her* in."

I wiped my mouth with the back of my hand.

"And you knew what it was?"

Suspicion tilted his chin upward and pursed his lips. He flicked his bangs out of his eyes with a sideways snap of his head.

All I could do was nod. My throat had narrowed to the circumference of a pinprick.

"How did you know?" he asked.

The question bubbled to the surface and widened his eyes once more.

"You didn't...?"

"No!" I cut him off before he spoke the words I could not bear to hear.

It sickened me that he would even think that I could kill someone and then dump them in the fucking garbage.

"I didn't do anything."

Patrick snapped his mouth shut and squinted at me. My legs gave out, and I slid to the floor, sobbing. Patrick squatted beside me, draping his bony arm around my shoulders. I felt cold.

"John, what did you see? Tell me. It's okay. I need to know."

His voice assumed such a soothing tone that I wanted to believe that everything really was okay. In that instant, I wanted to tell him everything. I tried to push the words out but they wouldn't go. I descended into panic mode.

Could I tell him everything? Should I tell him about Damien? Fuck. Something about Patrick wasn't right. I mean, other than the fact that he had dragged a dead body into his apartment and was keeping it in his bathroom for God only knows what. He seemed... different. Distant. Wrong. I mean, he always struck me as odd, like I said, but something seemed really off. Why wasn't he more upset? Shit, I didn't know.

I'm keeping Damien a secret, I told myself. *At least for now. Until he comes back to murder my ass.*

"John, there's a dead girl in my bathtub." Patrick looked from me, to the body, then back again.

He licked his lips and sighed. There was something reptilian about the gesture.

"Are you going to tell me what's going on, or am I..."

"Or are you what? Are you going to have to call the cops?" I managed to find my voice and it was surprisingly loud. "You're the one with the fucking dead body in your house. What are you going to do with it? Oh, God, what are you going to do with *her*?"

I kept thinking of that damn coyote story. And how fucking calm he was. Was that the beginning of a smile tugging at the corners of his lips? Bile rose up into my throat again.

"No, we're not going to the police," he said. "We're going to get through this, just me and you. I'm going to need your help, okay? Now, pull yourself together. I'm close enough to freaking out without you going ape shit."

He winked. He actually fucking *winked* at me.

Maybe the gravity of the situation hadn't hit him yet? Could that be possible? Was this guy really a psycho, or what? Shit. He definitely didn't seem like he was on the verge of a full-blown freak-out. He had been crying, I thought, but he seemed incredibly laid-back. It was more than a little creepy. I was scared on so many levels. My brain was just about to go on total lockdown.

"Patrick," I managed, through my tears, "I need to run across the street and do some self-medicating, you know? It's been a rough day."

He considered, searching my face for something. He didn't say anything for a minute while I cried and blew my nose.

"Go get your shit and bring it back here," he finally said. "Tell your mom that you're helping me build something and that you might be here for a couple of days."

"She's out in Burbank for the weekend."

I wasn't sure I liked where this was headed. And I probably shouldn't have told him that my mom wasn't home. I wasn't thinking too clearly at that moment.

"Good." He smiled. "So, go get your shit and get back over here ASAP, okay? Bring me something, would you, maybe a couple of joints or something mellow?"

He stood and hauled me up by the wrist. I had a brief vision of stepping outside and just taking the fuck off, calling the cops from a payphone or something (were there even any payphones left in L.A.?), and jetting out to my Grandma's house in the Valley.

"Oh," he said, staring into my eyes, reading my scrambled mind, "and no funny stuff or I will come looking for you." His steely eyes flashed through his blond bangs, like new quarters hit with a flashlight. "And I will find you."

JOHN

Saturday, July 8 —

Sunday, July 9

I was never an addict or anything. Don't get the wrong idea. Yeah, I sold a little, and I'd used various substances since I was eleven, but I was no junkie. I'd seen what addicts looked like, knew what happened to them, even saw one die as he shot up. I had also watched alcohol ravage my mom every day of my short childhood, and it scared the shit out of me. The whole addiction thing is fucked. It eats up lives and hardly ever spits them back out. I had enough shit working against me without having to deal with that noise. The only reason I sold was because it paid more than working at McDonald's, and my mom and I needed the cash. The situation with Patrick, though, shit, that had me using a whole lot more than ever.

Under the influence was the only way I could process the shit that was happening around me without totally losing my mind. It was so fucking sick, and not in that good slang way. When I got back to Patrick's loft, after grabbing my stuff from my place, he told me something that rocked my entire world. Also not in a good way.

When I opened the door to Patrick's place, he was nowhere in sight. His was a typical trendy loft kind of place, you know, with no walls separating the living, sleeping and kitchen areas, lots of brick and concrete. I looked around, scanning the stained corduroy sofa, the piles of rusty industrial junk and other assorted garbage, the high-end audio equipment, the unmade four-poster bed, the grungy stainless and granite kitchen, and, of course, the leering Frankenstein canvases. I closed the front door and started for the mammoth bookcase, which was completely jammed. It took up a third of the living space and contained dozens, maybe hundreds, of art books that I would have loved to check out. I reached for a Warhol bio and a hand grabbed my shoulder from behind. I jumped.

"Hey," I gasped.

Patrick stood behind me, smiling, a heavy book in his hand. It was an encyclopedia of taxidermy. I looked from its worn spine to his angular ashy face.

"John," he said, with a grin, "we've got work to do."

He raised his eyebrows in a way that would make Jack Nicholson jealous. The hairs on the back of my neck stood up. I felt again like I was trapped in a horror movie. Why didn't I run? Because I was a stupid-ass scared son-of-a-bitch, that's why. *Damn* it.

He flipped from his old taxidermy books to his Google results on 'embalming' and other ghoulish terms on the tiny laptop balanced on his knees. For a little while, he sat in the bathroom, on the toilet with the lid closed, staring at her. I did everything I could to hold my shit together, but, man, it was tough. While I stuffed my veins with one chemical, he plotted to fill hers with another.

By nightfall, he had rolled up his sleeves and really got to work. *We* got to work. He dragged a heavy plastic tarp into the living area. We hauled the super-heavy book-laden coffee table over to one side of the room and pushed the sofa back. We carried the stiff corpse in and laid it in the middle of the dropcloth. If I were religious, I would have prayed for her. And for him, too, the psychotic fuck, as he pierced that graceful neck with the first arterial tube.

Rubber tubing unceremoniously leaked the stream of her spent life into a gesso-spattered bucket. I could not pry my eyes from her beautiful face as Patrick preached the importance of draining her fluids. I wanted to see her sparkling cerulean eyes, but Patrick had secured her eyelids with masking tape.

What was Patrick's demeanor, you want to know? Well, I didn't want to think about it, to tell you the truth, because it was just so fucking bizarre. Patrick had always been pretty quiet and polite, you know? Kind of freaky, but not over-the-top psycho or anything. But, as he became more involved with the body, he became kind of, I don't know, manic or something. He was kind of sad that first day, but after that, he was more excited than anything. Every now and then I'd catch him standing over her, gazing down with this look, almost like he was in love with her. I'd seen him look at his girlfriend like that back when they were happy.

He also seemed like he really didn't give a fuck. About anything. Still. His face had hardened into a neutral mask of industrious determination. He sung a lot, mostly Nine Inch Nails or Violent Femmes tunes, some other stuff I didn't recognize.

After he had used some kind of electric pump thing to flood the girl's body with something called co-injection chemicals, and then an arterial fluid, we carried her back into the bathroom and put her in the tub. I folded her hands over her chest, like I'd seen in movies. I thought about putting a pillow under her head, but I didn't actually do it. I touched her cold cheek once, out of pity, I think, and Patrick yelled at me.

"John," he snapped, "don't touch it."

It. She was an *it* to him. Just another medium through which to express his own angst. I had been trying to think of a way out of the whole situation, but I'd been just too wasted and too scared to come up with any kind of coherent plan. I didn't know if I was more terrified of Patrick's shit or of the possibility of Damien hunting me down.

◇ ◇ ◇

I remember having to piss like a racehorse, but I really did not want to go into that bathroom anymore. Not with her in there. Just as I had been wishing for Patrick's place to suddenly grow a second bath, a thunderous pounding shook the front door.

My eyes flicked to Patrick. He gawked at me, mouth open.

"What do we do?" I asked in a stage whisper.

"Um..." He heaved a mildly irritated sigh and shrugged his shoulders. "I'll just go send whoever it is away." He smiled a little.

"What if it's the cops?" I so did not want to go to jail. Then, I had an even worse thought: what if it was Damien? I bit my tongue before that thought could slip out. I was extra paranoid from the blunt I'd just smoked, and I could feel my mind going numb, but I was totally in control of my tongue-biting faculties. My arms broke out in goose-bumps.

"John, relax, okay? I'll handle it."

He waved me into the bathroom and nonchalantly crossed to the front door. He even whistled as he went. 'Head Like A Hole,' I believe it was. Creepy.

And, so, I'd ended up in that bathroom anyway. I looked at the girl in the tub. I thought she looked... bigger. Maybe she was starting to swell a little. I worried for my soul, grabbed two ecstasy tabs from my pocket and dry swallowed them, then pressed my ear up against the door. I heard the front door swing open with a groan, accompanied by a woman's voice.

"Hello, darling," she said.

Patrick's ex-girlfriend? Nah, didn't sound like her. Besides, she'd dumped him. The raspy voice sounded older.

"Here, I picked up a few things for you at the market — and it's a good thing I did. Look at you."

The rattle of paper bags drowned out Patrick's response. My head floated to the ceiling, the bathroom rotated around me, a monochromatic carousel of charcoal colored marble and gunmetal concrete.

"You look absolutely emaciated!" the woman's voice accused.

Oh, my God, it hit me: it was...

"Thanks, Mom. You look great, too."

... his Mother! No way. *Too funny*, I thought, in my altered state.

"Daddy and I are so excited about your exhibition next week. What are you going to wear? God, Patrick, what is that smell?"

Windows swooshed opened. Then banged shut. I pictured Mom running around the perimeter of the living space, throwing the towering windows up, and Patrick, right behind her, slamming them down. I stifled an involuntary giggle. My mood was definitely improving.

"Do you have any candles or anything?" She kept right on chattering. "Anyway, I can't stay. I just dropped by to say hello. I have to get home before your father and hide the scotch — the Johnsons are coming over for dinner. We're so proud of you, honey."

The briefest pause before I heard Mom utter the fateful words: "May I use your loo before I go, dear? It's a tortuous ride to Malibu at this time of day, you know."

She was right. Sitting in traffic in L.A., even Sunday traffic, particularly on the 405, was bad enough without a distended bladder. Or so I'd heard — I'd never been up to Malibu on a Sunday, or any other day, actually.

I didn't know what to do. I panicked as much as I could in my altered state of mind. My hand glided across a great abyss, seemingly detached from the rest of my body, and pulled the door open, even as my mind screamed "*No, what are you doing, asshat?!*" I almost bumped into Patrick's heavy-set mother as I sidled into the living room area.

"Oh, hi! Are you a friend of Patrick's?"

She grabbed my hand and squeezed. She reminded me of Ronald McDonald, only shorter and with more make up. And her shoes may have been a tad smaller. My mind flipped to a picture of the Grimace and a little laugh escaped through my nose.

"I'm his mom, Helen."

"Hi, Helen. I'm John," I managed. I didn't know whether to laugh or cry or faint.

She strolled by me and shut the bathroom door.

"Whoa, dude," I said, flopping down on the couch, giggling.

"Why the hell did you come out of there? Where's the chick?"

Patrick whipped the bangs out of his eyes so hard I thought he'd need a neck brace. He bit down on his bent index finger, making cords in his neck stand out. It looked painful. This was more emotion than I'd seen from the dude since I'd barged in.

"Oh, yeah, well, she said thanks for the hospitality and all, but she had to bail."

Too bad the humor of the situation was lost on him in his descent into complete depravity.

"Chill, man, she's in the tub. I pulled the shower curtain. As long as your mom doesn't want to take a shower, she won't even know she's there."

He jerked his head to the side again and regarded me with a suspicious grunt.

"Why are you in such a good mood? A minute ago you were scared shitless."

"Better living through chemistry, my friend." I grinned. "Plus, your *mom* showed up, dude. How hilarious is that?"

I really did think that was the shit. Ping! You drag home a dead body and keep it in your bathtub and your mom stops over with hummus on her way home from Whole Foods! Priceless!

He glared at me. My smile faded.

A skein of silence spooled out between us, stretching longer and longer, tauter and tauter.

Flush.

Our eyes locked in silence. Sweat broke out on my palms, at my temples. His black-lined eyes bored into my forehead. Well, one eye — the other was covered by his platinum hair again.

Running water hissed.

Patrick and I watched each other's eyes in tense silence. I could hear the grinding of his teeth and a *poing* from my empty stomach.

The bathroom door flew open with a bang.

My heart dropped into my shoes.

"Jesus, Patrick! Next time I go shopping, I'd better buy you some Glade or something. I know it's that vegetarian diet of yours."

Never mind I was the one who had just come out of there. Patrick's old lady was funny.

"No time to chat," she blustered. "I've got to run. Like I said, the Johnsons are coming for dinner." She rolled her eyes at me, mimed taking a drink. "What are you going to wear next week? Did I ask you that already?"

Patrick opened the door for Helen. She looked over her shoulder at me, "'Bye, Josh!"

I waved and smiled. I felt damn near giddy.

"Honey, I love you, and Daddy and I will see you at the gallery."

She shot another glance at me, then said at a slightly lower, but still very audible, volume, "Will your friend be there? You're not gay now, are you? That would just kill your father."

Patrick sighed and shook his pale face no, eyes wandering to the ceiling.

"Okay, son, love you. Ciao! Kiss, kiss." And with that, poof, she disappeared.

Patrick shut the door, leaned his back on it and melted to the floor, bangs settling over both eyes.

JOHN

Monday, July 10

An Amber Alert had been issued for Mary Bellows, age six-teen, of Anaheim, California, last seen at the Hollywood Palladium, attending an In Dreams concert. Patrick and I watched the press conference on TV as we passed a fry (which, for the normal among you who wouldn't know that kind of thing, is a formaldehyde-dipped joint) back and forth, and he fiddled with the girl's flimsy clothing. She now had a name. *Day-um*. Hearing her actual name made it all too fucking real for me, triggered my fight-or-flight mechanism. I had to get the fuck out of there, man. My eyes flicked to Patrick's face. It reminded me of a shut-off TV.

The local Fox affiliate had a reporter at the Bellows' house, where, from the immaculate front lawn, Mary's highly distraught parents begged for any information at all regarding the whereabouts of their beloved daughter. They said that their little girl was the most special child in the world — a lover of music, a friend to animals, an honor student at one of the best private schools in the na-tion, and, please, whoever has her, please just bring her home. Through her tears, the mother croaked once again that Mary had attended the In Dreams concert at the Pal-ladium, in the company of her seventeen-year-old cousin, three nights ago. She held up a yearbook photo of the girl, scowling at the camera, black eyeliner so thick it looked almost like a mask. She was beautiful in the picture. And alive.

On TV, Mary's cousin, Kelly, stood behind and to the

right of the parents, her pudgy face set in a mildly annoyed expression. She looked inconvenienced. Her mouth worked as she chewed gum, busily snapping it, while one hand twisted itself in the short frizzy haystack that floated atop her fat head. At one point, I swear on my life, that wide bland face turned directly toward the camera, toward me. Pale fat sausage fingers curved around her smug mouth, thick berry lined lips formed distinct words: "I'll get you, John." And she smiled for half a second before returning to her disinterested gum-snapping stupor.

Christ, I was freaking out.

On some level, I had known that the girl — Mary — would be reported missing by someone. I was just not prepared to see it on television — the grieving sleep-deprived parents, the swarm of pushy journalists, the bumbling sheriff, the stuffed animal mountain topped with flowers and balloons on the lawn. I felt sick all over again. I sweated and shook, my teeth chattering like I was stranded in the middle of Antarctica in my swimsuit. Fueling an extreme edge of paranoia was the knowledge that they knew — *everyone* knew — that she had been at Damien's concert. I wondered how long it would take the cops to uncover the ugly truth of what had gone down yards from where I sat. I wondered how long it would take for them to come and arrest me. It was, without a doubt, in the pipeline.

I couldn't figure out why that girl's parents would let her go to a concert in Hollywood without an adult. Idiots. Didn't they know what happened to little girls who ventured out alone into the wilderness of Tinsel Town? Maybe they were drunks. Nah, that stuff didn't happen out in Orange County, where everyone was perfect and beyond rich. Ha ha, that's a joke. There were probably more alcoholics and drug addicts living in the O.C. than there were downtown. Seriously, though, they didn't look like the type. They looked gaunt and exhausted, zombie stick figures in matching Ralph Lauren polos. I don't think I'll ever get the sound of the mother's sobbing out of my head.

Talk about a total buzzkill. I had come so close to achieving a decent high before Patrick turned on the TV. A sharp pang of guilt pushed my eyes back over to where Mary lay on the tarp. Patrick knelt over her, studying the contours of her limbs, almost tracing their curves with the tip of his sharp nose. I felt like puking yet again. Damn, I thought I had that under control.

I had been scared, but then Patrick dropped the bomb on me.

He had this whole fucked up grand plan about how he could become instantly and unbelievably famous.

He showed me a book about an artist by the name of Damien Hirst. He was the one who floated that shark in a big tank full of formaldehyde and ended up selling it for something like seventeen million dollars. That shark made Hirst the world's most famous, not to mention loaded, contemporary artist. Of course I'd heard of him before, being an art freak myself, but I had only known about the shark and the mass-produced spot paintings. I had been blissfully unaware of the 'Beyond Belief' exhibition, until Patrick enlightened me.

According to the book that Patrick showed me, the show had been held at the famed White Cube and featured paintings of biopsied organs, dead sheep worshiping the silver skeleton of a baby in an incubator, and a full-sized human skeleton suspended in the middle of intersecting glass panes. The big draw was some poor asshole's skull covered in eleven hundred karats of near-perfect diamonds. That one piece alone later sold for — get this — *one hundred and eight point four million dollars*. No shit.

When he showed me that book, it hit me like a cattle prod to the nads. I understood, with acute clarity, what he meant to do with Mary Bellows.

Sure, Hirst's work was interesting, but Patrick took the guy's most twisted ideas and dove deeper, to obscene and criminal depths. Totally beyond twisted. I could not believe that Patrick — my friend, the vaguely creepy but friendly and encouraging neighbor — was really planning anything that fucking ghoulish. I felt like the bottom had dropped out of my world. Nothing seemed real. I was trapped in the worst nightmare I'd ever had. What was I doing there?

Looking at the book with Patrick, I have to admit, I was strangely intrigued by the images. Under more normal circumstances, I would have fallen in love with that shit right then and there. But, as it was, my mind was drawn to the more macabre practical aspect of the work. I wondered where Hirst had gotten the skull and the skeletons and the farm animals. The bones could have been cast from plaster or something, but he'd have to make a mold from real bones first, right? And the sheep and cows he used sure looked real to me. According to some animal rights nuts, they were. I could imagine him shooting a calf full of arrows, the heartbreaking mooing and bleating, the artist approaching as the life drained out of the animal, slipping in its blood, and then fitting the whole mess into a vitrine, shoving the arrows deeper into the flesh and grinding them around to make the whole gruesome thing fit in the glass box. I wasn't a vegetarian or anything, but the scenario I had conjured up brought tears to my eyes.

I wondered what Hirst would do if he found a dead body in the garbage. The thought made me shudder. I was always more of a Francis Bacon and Salvador Dali fan. Just paint on canvas, thanks.

Patrick desperately wanted what Hirst had achieved: fame, infamy, notoriety. I don't think he gave a shit about the money; his family had plenty. What he absolutely lusted after was immortality. He told me. And isn't that what every artist (actor, writer, rock star) wants?

Mary Bellows. Just a kid, meeting her idol at a concert, her dream turning into a nightmare. I began to realize that I was kind of mad at her. Didn't her parents ever tell her not to take rides with strangers? Didn't they care? I realized that I was pissed off at them. I shot Mary a fierce look. I felt like slapping her stupid porcelain face.

And Patrick. What did he do after we saw the press conference on TV? He chuckled and shook his head like someone had just told him a bad joke.

To be totally honest, I was really fucking scared — of Patrick, one of my best friends. My mind flashed back to how we used to hang out on the front steps and shoot the shit as the sun went down. Had that really been only four days ago? He used to tell me about art shows at exclusive galleries in Santa Monica that I would have been way too self-conscious and embarrassed to set foot in, in my dirty jeans and Black Sabbath T-shirts. I lived vicariously through that lucky dude. In return, I always filled him in on my neighborhood observations, who came to me to buy what, showed him some of my drawings. Give and take. I guess he had been my friend, in a way. I was still scared of him.

The one cool thing about Patrick, though, was that he always encouraged me to stick with my art. Always. No matter how crappy some of my stuff was. And he was the only one who had supported me. My mom thought art was a waste of time, dooming me to a life of poverty and unemployment — but, then again, she knew that that was my fortune, anyway. My teachers told me to get my head out of the clouds and focus on my drafting courses if I wanted to draw. I loved art, and I wanted so badly to make a career out of it someday, mostly because Patrick had told me that it was possible. I had started to believe him, even if only a little.

But, as things were turning out, maybe I didn't want to be like Patrick after all. If the slightest chance existed that pursuing art could drive me out of my mind and force me to such dark places, maybe I couldn't handle it. Maybe drafting blueprints would be better for me. Shit, maybe being shot dead in an alley over a bag of shitty coke cut with baking soda would be better. Now what was I supposed to do with my future?

I sat thinking about my murky future as Patrick smoked

cigarettes and studied photos in a science textbook that he had borrowed from the library. He looked different. Maybe it was because neither of us had slept much. He had this hollow look to him. Faded. I wondered if I had that same look. We were ghosts of the people we had been just a couple of days before.

"We need to get some supplies, Igor."

He had called me that a few times. Igor. I didn't like it. I didn't respond. I just looked out the window, trying to pretend I was somewhere else.

"I think I know where I can get some metal frames and glass, stuff to make my own vitrines," he said. "Time is of the essence. Even pumped full of chemicals, she's going to start to stink pretty soon." He bent close to her and sniffed. "Tick tock." He leered at me.

I don't know how he could have been so cheerful, or enthusiastic, or whatever you want to call it. I had thought about calling the cops a bunch of times, but I was really scared of going to jail. Yeah, I know, I was a juvenile and all that, but I didn't know about a case like this. We had murder, conspiracy, planning to make artwork out of a missing body — I don't know what they called that kind of thing, but I was sure it had to be a big deal. I hadn't been prepared to give up my freedom. I hadn't realized that it had already been stolen from me.

Patrick had confiscated my cell.

"Hey, Patrick? Can I have my phone? I really need to call my mom."

Yeah, he was keeping me from talking to anybody. When I told him that I was not cool with that, he had me assign a different ringtone to my mom's number and said I could answer calls that came from her. I still didn't like it, but it was better than nothing.

"Yeah, grab it off the counter. I'll dial the number for you."

The bastard. He was that worried about me calling the cops. My phone lay on the granite next to the black dog collar that had been around Mary's neck. It creeped me out to even have to go near that thing. I snatched the phone and gave it to Patrick to dial. I held it to my ear and started toward the opposite side of the huge room.

"Hey, uh-uh, you stay where I can hear you," he said to my back.

I turned and caught the mistrust in his glassy eyes as he flicked his head to rearrange his hair. It made me shiver. Was he even in there anymore? And that flicking of his head, to clear the bangs out of his eyes, was starting to drive me a little nuts. Had he always done that? Was it some kind of nervous tic or what? Maybe dude should get a haircut, I thought. My mom picked up on the third ring.

"Hi, Mom. How's Grandma?"

She had stayed on in the Valley, taking care of her mom for a few more days. She didn't know that I'd been at Patrick's since she left.

"Hi, Hon. Grandma's okay. Her ankles are a little swollen and they're talking about putting her on dialysis, but she's hanging in there. I'll tell her you say 'hi.'"

She sounded fairly relaxed, which was unusual.

"Yeah, good. Listen, Mom, if you call and I don't pick up, just leave a message, okay? I kind of have a cold, so I'm going to try to get some rest."

I perched on the arm of a worn brown leather club chair and stared at the red-and-cream Persian rug beneath my feet.

"You don't sound stuffy. Do you want me to come home? I can come tonight, if you're really not feeling good."

I thought she was looking for an excuse to dump Grandma and come home to good ol' Jack Daniels.

"No, Mom, really, I'm okay. I just wanted to let you know that I was here, just not answering the phone, you know?"

I sniffled for effect, feeling Patrick's eyes on me. I wasn't fooling anybody.

"Take care of Grandma and I'll see you on Wednesday

night or whatever."

Patrick listened to the whole thing, eyes bolted to my lying face. He probably thought I was going to try to send some secret message or something, like fucking James Bond or some shit. Whatever, dude. I gave him my phone after I hung up.

"Okay, Igor, listen up."

He held the Hirst book in front of me, open to the shark in the tank.

"I need to make a vitrine, like this, only smaller."

"Dude, you can't just leave her whole like that! Are you damaged? And stop calling me fucking Igor."

I furrowed my brow and grimaced at him.

He rolled his eyes and snorted. "I know I can't leave her whole, dipshit. But I can use pieces, you know? Kind of float some of them like this, hold them in place with wire. Nobody's going to know that they're real. Who'll be able to tell? I'll make them into other stuff, like animals or something."

"That's messed up. This whole thing is messed up."

The words flew out of my mouth before I could stop them. I did not want to piss him off, seeing how he had turned into a total fucking psycho, but that ship had kind of sailed by that point. I could not get my head around what he was doing.

"Why the fuck are you doing this, man? Did you see her parents, dude? She's someone's kid. They loved her."

I looked him in the eye, thinking what my mom might do when they found me chopped up in a fish tank. He heaved an overly dramatic sigh and looked away. Then, he walked over to where I sat on the sofa and planted himself on the arm.

"John, this is it. This is my big break, my ticket to the big time."

He looked into my eyes and then up to the ceiling, like he was trying to think of how to explain death to a little kid.

"Listen," he sighed, moving his eyes back to my face. "I'll make you rich. Okay? How about that? John, you're my friend, kid. Help me with this, do this with me, and you can have all the money." He arched his eyebrows at me. "No shit. Every penny. I just really, really need this. I know you don't understand, but, please, I promise, you can have the money. Take it all and move out of that shithole you live in before anything really bad happens to you."

He stopped talking long enough to take a drink from the bottle of Snapple iced tea that sweated in his hand.

"But, dude, this is my fifteen minutes. I gotta take it."

I took a deep breath and exhaled like I was blowing up a balloon. He knew that I dealt drugs so that I could eat and buy shoes. He didn't know that I snuck money into my mom's purse to help out with the bills and the rent, though. Man, it would be nice to quit selling poison to other kids and move my mom out to a nice safe neighborhood, maybe Encino or someplace. I ran my hands through my mop of hair and looked down at my grimy jeans. Something told me to get up, cross the room, and just walk out. But, something else screamed at my immature brain to take the deal, accept it as my ticket out of destitution. The latter something proved louder, stronger, and way more persuasive.

"Christ, man, what choice do I have?"

I templed my hands and cupped them over my nose and mouth, exhaling with force. I rubbed my hands together and crossed my arms.

"I rat on you and we'll both be toast. You'll probably tell the cops about my dealing and everything. I'm not stupid."

My guts knotted up, my palms sweated, a lump formed in my throat. I was truly torn. Should I dig my heels in, take the high ground and risk going to prison (or getting killed) while Mom drinks herself to death, or let it all go and enjoy the ride to the good life? What kind of choice was that? What kind of kid was I? I chose the only real option.

"I know you're not stupid. I also know that you're just a kid."

Patrick walked over to the kitchen and dropped my phone on the polished granite counter.

"Look, I'm really sorry that you're involved in this. I don't know why you even came over here in the first place. You should have stayed away, man."

He actually looked sorry. For a second.

He had no idea that I was worried about Damien finding me. He had no fucking clue about how much trouble I thought I was in. I had absolutely nowhere to go. He was offering me something I'd always needed, something that would give my life some stability. Being fifteen and vulnerable, I hadn't considered the cost.

The cost? Freedom? Silence? My soul? While I could not predict the actual cost, the toll it would take on my sanity, the radical and irreversible changes it would bring to my life, I knew it would be huge.

"Yes," I mumbled.

"What?"

I took a deep breath.

"I'll help you. Look, I don't know if you know this, but... I want to get out of this fucking neighborhood. Before my mom and I get kicked to the curb, you know? Before I get hit by a stray bullet. I know you don't see it, but bad shit happens around here. You don't notice it because all you artsy types lock yourselves in your pretentious lofts and say, 'oooh, look how dark and gritty real life is.'" I chuckled. "I see what's going on around here — sure, things are getting better — less crime, more Starbucks, whatever. But did you ever notice how the poor people are getting forced out by you rich fucks who want these fancy lofts and more coffee places?"

I waved my arm around Patrick's palatial apartment, pointed toward the wall of windows, which were draped in black velvet so no one could see inside.

"No, of course, you don't notice that. Why would you?"

I looked down at my worn sneakers.

"Hey, I gotta do what I gotta do, right?"

I wiped my runny nose on the back of my hand.

He strolled over to me and shook my hand, clapped me on the shoulder, grinning.

"You're a good kid, John."

I wasn't so sure about that.

He grabbed his keys and headed for the door.

"Well, I'm going down to this glass place before it closes. You sit tight, and don't leave unless the building's on fire."

I'd have felt like a hostage if he'd said that a few minutes before, but the sudden prospect of actually making some serious coin from this ungodly situation had lit a tiny pinpoint spark of optimism somewhere within me. Maybe things would be okay. Maybe I could handle it.

"Hey, um, I have to run back across the street and feed my mom's cat, but I'll come right back, okay?"

Yeah, it was a lie, but I had to get out of there, at least for a few minutes, to clear my head, to think about what I was doing, to take a look at how shitty my life was and to say goodbye.

Patrick didn't look too happy. He looked kind of nervous.

"Okay, but make it quick, and be sure to come right back."

He went back to the kitchen and gave me a key from a hook on the wall.

"Here. Hurry up, and I'll be back in a while."

On his way out the door, he turned and stared at me.

"Trust," he said, pointing his index finger at me like a gun, poking me in the chest.

We left the building, and I raced across the street, glad to be free, if only for a moment.

I let myself in and stood in the middle of the tiny living room. I looked around at the objects my mom and I had scrounged up in an effort to make our miserable life a smidge more comfortable: the ugly orange sofa, scarred with brown ringed cigarette burns, listing to one side because it was missing a leg; the giant twenty-six inch stone-age TV with actual knobs on it; a dreary Monet print in a black plastic frame, hanging on the wall, covering a hole in the drywall; the white fiberboard bookcase, crammed with plastic-jacketed books that had been bought for quarters at library sales. It was dark in that apartment even though the sunlight streamed through the picture window, unfiltered. The rays never dissipated the dank gloom that hung over the collection of empty liquor bottles and piles of dirty laundry. I couldn't believe we'd be getting out of there. It seemed way too good to be true. I'd miss the place, I thought, for some strange and incomprehensible reason. I pondered the sensation as I lit up the crack pipe that I'd always kept hidden behind the bookcase.

I hadn't been in the apartment for more than ten minutes when there was a loud bang on the door. I jumped almost right out of my clammy skin. My heart thrashed against my sternum. I looked at the scorched pipe in my hand and quickly shoved it in a kitchen drawer.

"Who is it?" I yelled across the tiny room.

Through the cheap-ass door, I heard the four-letters I dreaded more than any others:

"L.A.P.D."

Holy shit, this was it! This was where I went down, where it all fell apart. So much for my suburban future. It wasn't quite the goodbye I'd had in mind.

PATRICK

Monday, July 10

So, the glass place had everything I needed, including the metal framing to hold the panels in place.

"You want me to help you carry this in, dude?" the truck driver asked.

He'd given me a ride back to my place. Nice guy. Good customer service. I'd use them again, were I not going to jail.

"No, thanks, I'll get my friend."

I ran up the steps and threw open the front door. Gil was at the front desk, texting someone on his phone and chewing gum with his mouth open. I flew up to my apartment.

"John?"

I looked around the open space. Not a soul in sight. I checked the bathroom. No souls there, either, but *it* was still in the bath tub where I left it. Where the fuck was that kid?

I skipped down the steps to the lobby and confronted Gil.

"Hey, man, come help me carry some stuff, would you?"

Gil heaved a sigh, like I was asking him to help me push an elephant into a Volkswagen or something. Lazy sod. I watched him round the marble-topped desk and open the front door for me. Then I led him outside.

"Holy shit, that's a lot of glass," Gil said, chomping on his bubblegum. "Gonna be pretty damned heavy."

Angling for a tip already. Bastard.

We unloaded all of the supplies and carried them up to my place. As I was sorting the pieces of glass by size and leaning them carefully against the wall, Gil disappeared.

"Hey, you haven't said anything about my Franken..."

That's when I looked up and noticed he was missing. I also noticed the bathroom door was open.

Fuck.

I crossed to the bathroom with a small pane of glass still in my hands.

He stood there gaping at her. His wad of gum sat on the floor, just in front of his dull black wingtip. He must've heard me walk in because he turned my way.

"What the fuck is this? What are you doing? I gotta call the cops."

That was the last thing poor old Gil ever said.

I smashed the pane of glass on the countertop and drove a shard into ol' Gil's throat before he could get his phone out of its holster. He sank to his knees as blood sprayed from his neck and bubbled from his mouth. He was still trying to talk, but all that came out was a big bubble of blood — a bubble bigger than one he could've made with his wad of gum. It popped and splattered my shirt. Then he turned his head and just showered me with gore. It was ugly. He was able to catch one last glimpse of himself in the mirror before he fell to the floor and bled out.

What a fucking mess that was. He ruined not only my favorite Abercrombie & Fitch Beaver Point shirt, but also a pair of Indian Falls cargo shorts, about four-hundred dollars' worth of towels, and one bamboo bathmat. Plus, I had to clean everything up before the cops came knocking.

Oh, and I had two dead bodies in my apartment instead of just one. The good news was I didn't think anyone would miss Gil. He was never at the front desk anyway.

JOHN

Monday, July 10

My eyes rolled around, my heart drummed faster and harder than Keith Moon on crystal meth. I was a rabbit caught in a bear trap. Fuck a duck.

The door pounded again. I stood up straight, inhaled as deeply as possible, and exhaled in a coughing fit.

"I'm coming," I shouted, trotting the few steps across the living room, grabbing a pair of shades off the kitchen counter as I blew by.

They were my mom's Gucci knockoffs and looked most definitely girly. They had some swirly fake diamond shit on the sides and everything, but I didn't have time to worry about that. I cracked the door and had a badge thrust under my nose.

"What can I do for you, officer?"

This was it. This was my brain on meltdown. Not only was I a witness and an accessory to a crime (or crimes), but I also absolutely reeked of weed. Oh, and, of course, I'd be remiss if I didn't mention that I was fucking high on crack!

"Hi. Detective O'Brien." The badge flew away. "I'm just in the neighborhood, asking some questions. You got a minute?"

"Uh, sure."

I opened the door a fifth of a hair wider and willed my mouth into something approximating a U-shape. Ohmygodohmygodohmygod. What should I do? Should I tell him the truth? Here was my chance to 'fess up, duck out of the whole scene with minimal damage. The guy totally looked like that old Grissom dude, from 'C.S.I.' — curly gray hair, wire-rimmed glasses. I crushed the sudden urge to laugh by biting the side of my tongue. Fucking unreal.

"Um... you live here? Your parents home?"

The detective's mud-colored eyes narrowed as they scanned down my faded Buzzcocks T-shirt to my yellowed fingertips gripping the edge of the door. I tried to hold my breath in a futile attempt to keep at least one of my noxious odors to myself.

"Yeah, I live here. My mom's not home, sorry."

I stood up straight and fixed my eyes on the fire alarm across the gloomy pissy hallway, over the cop's square shoulder. Nope, I won't spill it, I decided. I wanted a better life. I wanted it — no, *needed* it, no matter what I had to do.

The detective sent his penetrating cop glare past my own scrawny shoulder, through the trashy apartment, assessing what he could of the kitchen and living areas. Empty liquor bottles and dirty clothes decorated most horizontal surfaces. He shifted his intense stare to my eyes, which were, without a doubt, behind the sparkly diva shades, red and glassy.

He inhaled through his stuffy nose and barked a single wet cough.

"You been drinking, son?"

"Oh, uh, no, sir. That's, um, my mom's stuff."

Embarrassment heated my face. It sounded suspicious even to my untrained intoxicated teen ears. I really hoped the guy sucked at his job. He looked over his shoulder and then back at me. I wondered if he pitied me. He had that kind of look. I hated that shit, man. Someday people would not look at me that way.

"Mind if I wait for her to get back? I need to talk to her."

Cool as a penguin at the Pole. Shit. Possible bright spot: he sounded like he had a most gnarly cold.

"Uh, yeah, well, I don't know how long she's going to be."

I needed a way to get rid of the dude. A feeble plan bubbled to the surface of my unreliable consciousness.

"And, to tell you the truth, I kind of have the runs, so, you know... I gotta go to the bathroom."

I know it was lame — I was under a lot of pressure, so piss off.

"Maybe it would be better if you came back later. If that's okay, I mean."

I bent my knees a little and bobbed up and down, like I was doing my damnedest to keep my sphincter shut.

That freaking cop would not get lost. He looked at me funny and kept right on talking.

"Where did she go?"

He sniffed again at the stale air. I hoped like hell he had a sinus infection because only a butt-load of mucus could keep him from smelling the pot on my clothes.

I bobbed faster, out of total desperation.

"Well, she's taking care of her mom, you know? Grandma just started dialysis and she's super old and sick, and..."

"And you live here, right?"

Christ, didn't we cover that already?

"Yes, sir, and I really have to go..."

No dice. The fucker would not move.

"How long have you lived here? And what's your name, son?" he asked, raising a caterpillar of an eyebrow.

He fished a pen and a little yellow pad of paper out of his worn blazer.

"Um, about six years, maybe seven. My name is John. John Thomas."

He wrote it down. Great. I was already wishing that I'd been smart enough to lie.

"Do you, by any chance, know a Mr. Jeffrey Cole?"

I quit bobbing and stood up straight. I squinted and rubbed my chin, trying to look like I was thinking instead of totally losing my fucking mind.

"Oh. Um, I don't know. Does he live around here?"

Fuck, he knows. He knows!

"Across the street. You know him? Jeff Cole?"

Fuck, he knows *everything*! I bobbed faster than before, like a piston in a racing engine. I thought I looked like I was in total agony. But maybe I was a shitty actor — ha ha, pun intended. He stared through my shades, maybe trying to probe my mind or doing some Jedi mind trick shit. I stared back, willing him to leave or to at least have a stroke.

"Jeff Cole..."

I scratched my head.

He glared at my artificially yellow hair.

"Better known as Damien Tungsten," he said.

He pulled out a whitish rag and blew his nose with a mighty wet honk. I hopped from one foot to the other, sucking breath through my clenched teeth, hoping he'd hurry the fuck up. It was highly doubtful, but I was no quitter.

Nothing. Maybe he figured he wouldn't be able to smell anything, anyway, just in case I wasn't lying and really did shit my pants.

"You know him or not? Damien Tungsten?"

"Yeah, sure, he lives across the street. Everybody knows him. He's in that faggot boy band."

I frowned and stuck out my tongue.

"Yep, that's the one."

The cop grinned as though he agreed with my assessment of the band's sexuality.

"When's the last time you saw him?"

"Um, I really don't remember. Couple days ago, maybe."

Shit. My heart was pumping like mad. Maybe I'd get lucky and die of a heart attack right on the spot.

"Two days? Three? Five? What would you say?"

I hated cops.

"Hmmm... I don't know. I don't really know. I don't really see him that often, so it's hard to say. I don't really know him. I think he's got an ego problem, if you ask me."

I was lying. I felt like Spongebob, in that episode where he cheats on his driver's test and screams "I'm cheating!" over and over, to his teacher.

The cop gave a little snort.

"Well, in your best estimate, what would you say?"

"Ummm... maybe four days ago."

I'm lying! my mind screamed at the cop.

"Guess I'd be better off asking the girls around here, huh?"

He chuckled, but his eyes never left mine.

I felt tiny pinpricks of icy sweat on my back. I really did have to take a dump, by that point.

"Listen, you know anything about Tungsten and what's in the papers? About him missing?" the cop asked.

"I don't read the papers."

"You watch TV?"

"Um, sure. Oh," I smacked my forehead. "You know, I heard he's in rehab or something. Isn't he?"

"You ever see him use drugs, buying them maybe, maybe just talking to anyone suspicious-looking? Seen him with any girls recently?"

Oh, boy. *Stay cool*, I told myself. *Do not pass out.*

"Um... nope. I hardly ever see the guy."

My stomach let out this deep grinding sound.

The cop furrowed his brows.

"Sorry. Don't know anything about him really. And I've never seen him with a girl. I thought he liked guys."

Heh-heh. I threw that in just for kicks. Fucking Damien. If I ever see that prick again, he'd better just fucking run, that's all I got to say, putting me through all this shit.

"Okay."

The cop seemed far from satisfied.

"I gotta get back to work. Tell your mom I'll be back in the next couple of days. I might have some more questions for you, too, so don't go anywhere, got it?"

He handed me a card with his name and contact info

on it. Detective William P. O'Brien, Los Angeles Police Department, blah, blah. Grissom.

"Yes, sir."

I watched him walk away.

He glanced over his shoulder at me once, but kept moving toward the stairs.

That was it, I was committed, in it 'til the end.

He stepped out of view, and I shut the front door.

Then I ran to the bathroom.

Can I get a 'whew'?

JOHN

Monday, July 10 —

Tuesday, July 11

Patrick was not the least bit rattled by my visit with old Grissom. Said he'd been expecting it and that it was only a matter of time before the cops showed up at his place. And what did you know, there were a couple of local TV news vans parked around the corner when I came back across the street to his place. Word had gotten around that Damien had abandoned his tour in order to enter some rehab facility (*'allegedly'* entered rehab, I should say). They were all hoping to catch the prick when he came home. The media was not aware of any connection between Mary Bellows and Damien Tungsten at that point. Not that they announced, anyway. The cops sure suspected something, though.

Patrick was super-stoked because the owner of the art gallery where he was scheduled to have his show called and asked him to start moving in his work a little early. Some of the local critics wanted to see it before the opening so they could do an early write-up. Mr. Fawlty, the gallery owner, thought that would be just splendid free publicity for Patrick, not to mention for his own snotty gallery.

Not only that, but did I mention he'd acquired an extra body while I was across the street? Yeah! I had to get the fuck out of that place. You know what he did? He fucking cut the doorman into pieces and put the parts in his gigantic Sub-Zero freezer! He said the cops could deal with him later! No shit, man. Trip out.

Mary was laid out in front of us, designer clothes balled up in the corner. Poor O.C. Barbie girl. Patrick knelt beside her, a selection of gleaming metal tools fanned out around him. He trailed his index finger from the hollow at the base of her throat down to her navel. He looked up at me with a chilling expression of pure evil and beckoned me with a come-here/bangs-clearing snap of his head.

I swallowed hard and crawled over to him. He held a tool in his outstretched hand, offering it to me like he was passing me a lit joint. Light glinted off the razor sharp edge. It was a scalpel.

"Because you are my friend and I want to share the joy of my art with you," Patrick said in a terrifyingly gentle tone, "I want you to make the first cut. Go ahead, John. Destiny awaits."

He stared into my face.

It was scary.

My hands were slick with cold sweat as I took the knife from him. I knelt beside him and literally froze. I flashed back to the time I'd gone skiing in Tahoe and saw snow for the first time. I had never been so cold in my life. Until now. Patrick took my free hand, and with my index finger, he traced a line from the hollow at the base of the girl's throat slowly down to the very edge of the dark tangle of her pubic hair. Bile rose in my throat. The scalpel slipped from my trembling sweaty fingers.

I tried to concentrate on the money. That was going to be sweet. Our very own house. Maybe we'd even have a pool. I'd definitely go skiing again, maybe even buy my own skis.

With an aggravated sigh, Patrick shoved the scalpel back into my unsteady hand and guided the point to Mary's throat. When I still didn't move, he pressed my hand and the tip of the blade pierced her skin. I gasped and pulled my hand away, jumping to my feet, nearly slashing Patrick's face.

"Goddamnit, John! What are you trying to do, kill me?"

If only I'd thought of that first.

"I... I..."

The room whirled around me and I sat down hard on the plastic-covered concrete floor. Patrick plucked the scalpel from my fist and glared at me.

"Fuck it," he said. "I'll do it myself. I knew you wouldn't have the grapes. Fucking mama's boy."

And with that, Patrick zipped Mary's torso open with a flourish of his wrist and began his work, whistling 'Gone, Daddy, Gone' the whole time.

I crawled to the coffee table and rummaged through my opiate stash. It seemed like an opportune time to cook up and numb my screaming swirling mind as quickly as possible. I dumped some powder into a spoon and held it over a candle flame, squirted a couple drops of water in and stirred with the end of a match. It was my only escape. I thought about OD'ing on purpose, but then I realized my body would be left unprotected there with that sick fuck, so I scrapped that idea. I shot up and nodded on the couch, ignoring Patrick, retreating into the safe cocoon of my skull.

PATRICK

Tuesday, July 11

Vagus, baby, vagus. It's the nerve that makes you feel like puking after you get punched in the nose or break a bone or something. It's what makes people pass out in stressful situations, too. Large and in charge, that sucker runs all the way from your medulla oblongata down deep into your belly. It rules, among other things, gastrointestinal peristalsis. It's John's vagus nerve that makes him heave every time I sink my blade.

And, it's part of the thick cord I just stripped from our subject here.

It took some work to get this particular thread out. I had to dig around the subclavien artery, the superior vena cava, and a whole intricate tangle of other wires and hoses. Not bad for someone who's never studied medicine. If I had it to do all over, maybe I'd go to med school. There is some cool shit in the human machine. Anyway, the nerve itself is pretty impressive, lengthwise. It's kind of skinny and thready, but it'll look fucking brilliant when I loop it around the dice and poker chips in the vitrine.

"Vagus, baby, Vagus."

Excellent.

John is acting like a total fucking baby. The kid'll never get anywhere with that shitty attitude. I keep offering him the chance to create something out of this beautiful all-natural priceless material, but, damn it, he just does not appreciate this singular amazing opportunity. I've even got spare parts now! He whines about wanting to be an artist, yet there he sits, gutting his mind with the Jack the Ripper of drugs, letting this chance of a lifetime just drift away. When he's my age and no one wants to buy his heartfelt sketches of dogs and the Hollywood sign, maybe he'll recognize what he could have done here. I pity him already, knowing that emptiness. I sincerely hope that the money will be enough for that poor kid.

Ha! A fruit roll-up.

That's what that piece over there reminds me of. Purple, thick, dry, kind of leathery. I could pull a strip off and eat it right now, were I that sort of fiend. But I'm not. Sadly, I'm a vegan. It does look strangely appetizing, though, sandwiched between two plates of glass, light streaming around its pinkish translucent edges. Some collector will surely love it.

Let me tell you, it was a total bitch getting a slice that thin, though. I used a vegetable peeler first, but that just didn't yield a big enough slice. So I got out the old trapezoidal cheese grater my mother gave me, the one that looked, like, fifty years old or something, and that worked ever so much better. Tough object to work with, the lung. The advantage it has over other internal organs is its size. It's quite a bit larger than, say, the spleen or kidneys. But it's also tougher. And it looks like our subject was a smoker, so there's a little discoloration, which affects the purity of my statement. But that's alright, I suppose. It has to be, doesn't it?

The intestines were my favorite, I must say. After I had mined the thorax, I plundered a bit lower and freed the long rope of the digestive system. They say that, fully cut and flattened appropriately, the intestines will cover an area equivalent to a tennis court. With that bit of information in mind, I worked my knife along the length of the tube, carefully trimming it into sections, and then I stitched the rectangles into a sort of peritoneal quilt. And, of course, I have enough material to duplicate the larger rectangle, which I will then sew to the first one, and then stuff the resulting digestive duvet with something fluffy, perhaps hair, though I'll be surprised if there's enough. I may have to augment the hair with curls of dried skin. I don't know, we'll see. It will be absolutely mind-blowing.

People dream of reanimating the flesh of the newly deceased. It was one of H. P. Lovecraft's favorite themes, wasn't it? Ah, the sentimental fools. They have it all so wrong.

The human body is at its most beautiful once it is finally still.

That is when it truly becomes Art.

JOHN

Wednesday, July 14

Sometime later I became aware of Patrick talking at me from the edge of the tarp, the periphery of my massive internal void.

"Hey, check this out."

He held up what looked like a slide for a giant microscope. I blinked my eyes and tried to focus. A paper thin, translucent swatch of pink and purple veined tissue clung to the glass.

"I'll hang a series of these, and call it something like 'Hey! Wait! I Got a New Complaint.' What do you think?"

He looked proud. There was no other word to describe his expression.

I lolled on the sofa, trying to lift my leaden head. Patrick's level of excitement over chopping up a dead body totally creeped me out. Do I even need to say that? God, how did I get mixed up in that shit? I felt like I was losing my mind. The drugs had numbed me, though. I could just barely deal. As long as I didn't look at anything up close.

"Original," I croaked.

Heart tissue. From a real body. Holy Christ. I needed some air to clear my head and wake up.

"I'm gonna take a quick smoke break outside."

"Hey, take the garbage, would you? That pizza box is starting to reek, man. Oh, and you're not thinking about going anywhere, are you?"

The smile slipped across Patrick's thin lips like mercury as his surgical steel eyes crawled across my face.

"I just need some air."

I wondered how long it would take for the cops down the hall, who had finally descended in droves on Damien's place, to investigate the chemical smell wafting from Patrick's loft.

"Okay." He smiled.

He seemed okay, even though he had changed the locks on the apartment so he could lock me in when he went out.

"Oh, before you step out, I want to ask you something. A favor."

He looked at me earnestly.

"I really want you to do something for me. I mean, just in case something happens to me or anything, you know?" He sighed.

I didn't think I wanted to hear this.

"I want you to keep a few of these pieces."

"Um, look, Patrick," I began, not wanting to alarm him or give him any reason to hack me up. "I've, um, really seen enough."

Too fucking much.

"I'll really just need out once we're done here. I mean, yeah, I'll take the money, to get my mom out of here and get our lives straight, but... I don't want to get caught, you know? I just want to go away and forget all of this, like a bad trip."

He looked sad, like I had just told him I didn't want to be his friend anymore or something. Actually, that was what I was saying, now that I think about it.

"I hear you, bro." He nodded as he studied his ragged nails. "But, John, the reason I want you to have a few pieces is not for you," he said. "It's so that I can have a show later on and get what's coming to me. And that's where a lot of your money will come from, you know?"

Hmm. I couldn't argue with that. A second show would probably make way more money than the first just because of the hype factor.

"I know this is some really risky shit," he continued. "When it all comes out, people are going to think I'm Satan, and let's face it," he snorted, "I probably am."

He didn't seem to hate the thought.

"But, I need this. This is my ticket to immortality. All you have to do is keep the key to this self-storage facility where I rented a locker, and then take the vitrines to the gallery after the chips fall. That's it. It should fetch a sizable fortune, especially if I'm on death row or something. I don't give a fuck about the money, John."

He looked right into my soul.

"Just make sure my name is on the booklet. It's my show, my fifteen minutes."

I didn't know what to say. I needed to think. He was right; if I wanted the cash, I'd have to do some work, I guess. Shit. I was trapped. Again.

"You know they're right down the hall, right? The cops, I mean," I said.

I wondered if Patrick even knew what was going on anymore. He was pretty much batshit by that time, or so I thought. We never talked about the Amber Alert or anything. He never even mentioned Damien. We had stopped watching television. He had to have been thinking about something other than a fucking art exhibition, though, didn't he? I wondered if he was scared. Not that I particularly cared, but I was curious.

"I know. And that cop, the one who came to see you, is going to come knocking on my door any minute." He smiled at the floor. "I know I'm going to jail, John. And I can handle that. Yes, I can. But, please, just say you'll do this last show for me when I'm locked up? Kind of a posthumous event, only I won't exactly be dead. Yet."

He walked to the kitchen counter, grabbed something small and pressed it into my palm. It was a key.

"Dude," I said, heading for the door, "I need a cigarette and some fresh air. I'll be back in a minute."

I looked at the key.

"Don't forget the garbage," Patrick said over his shoulder.

Since he had returned to Mary's husk and wasn't watching me, I grabbed my phone off the counter as I passed through the kitchen.

I didn't see a single soul as I exited the building's back door and stepped into the alley. I leaned against the cool rough bricks and let out a sigh. I could not believe any of the shit that was happening. The sky was a purple haze millions of miles above my head. I wished I was on the moon.

I had to get away from this crazy shit. If I went to the cops, they could protect me. I mean, really, what was my role in all of that up to this point? I witnessed a murder. I then witnessed someone stealing the body — but was that really stealing? I confronted the body thief. I witnessed said thief 'interacting' with the corpse (*hacking her up* just sounded way too incriminating).

Ah, shit, I helped him fucking embalm her. And I lied to the cops. And I was a peeping Tom. Oh, yeah, and I just happened to run a DIY pharmacy. They had it all the fuck over me.

But, you know, behind my eyelids, I kept seeing Mr. and Mrs. Bellows, in their freshly pressed designer clothes, crying. They really missed their kid. I felt so bad. Man, that girl had parents who actually cared about her, and she threw it all away. For what? One lousy night with Damien Tungsten. Shit. Was Patrick going to make her famous? Maybe, but what would she really get out of the whole fucked up deal? Could I really take the money made from her hellish end and live with myself for sixty, seventy years? God, what was wrong with me?

My mental self-flagellation ground to a screeching halt as a car skidded to a stop inches from my toes. The right rear tire nearly dragged over my feet.

WTF?

Rough hands grabbed my upper arm, a handful of my

shirt. I heard the stitches popping loose.

No, what...

My head was shoved down and forward, thrust into the doorframe. Fireworks exploded somewhere inside my skull, instantly focusing my mind on the pain. I was thrown into the backseat of an old Cadillac. It smelled like cigarettes and fear. Or maybe that was me. We sped away from the alley.

Away from Patrick.

And Mary.

Flash.

JOHN

Wednesday, July 14

The only thing that sobers me up faster than watching the dismemberment of a human body is getting fucking kidnapped.

"My holy Christ, was exciting, no!"

The guy who grabbed me sunk into the rich-but-cracked leather, out of breath and laughing. Apparently, English was not his first language, and it was clear that he did not exercise regularly. Other than that, I had no idea who this fuck was. I involuntarily slid toward the sinkhole his fat ass made in the lumpy bench seat. A cigarette stuck to his beefy lips and bounced up and down in time with his bloated gut and sagging jowls as he chuckled. He smelled rotten. He was maybe in his fifties and massive. With his crooked beak and black hair, I guessed he was Italian. And that's never a good thing.

The driver, another older ethnic-looking guy, practically stood on the gas pedal, eyes wide, mouth in a full-on grimace. Beads of sweat glittered in his greasy black hair as he careened the car around a corner. He yelled some gibberish at the other guy in a language that did not sound like Italian — or even Spanish, for that matter — and they busted out laughing. Who the fuck were these guys?

We tore down Figueroa and forged a path through heavy traffic.

OhmyGodI'mbeingkidnapped!

My mouth hung open, and I stared out the window, watching office buildings, jewelry shops, and smoothie stands whiz by. I flashed on my mom, passing out with a cigarette burning down to her fingers. Who would save her when I was gone?

After what seemed like years of weaving through steady traffic and narrowly missing bike messengers and pedestrians, we got hung up at a red light. Big Man casually poked me in the ribs with the snub-nosed barrel of a shiny handgun. Don't ask me what kind. I had never been that close to an actual gun in my life. I was nearly shitting my pants. For real. What the hell was up with all this weird shit happening to me? I was totally freaking out.

The driver studied my sweaty face in the rearview mirror.

"You John?" he asked.

My name came out sounding like it started with a D.

I didn't say anything until Big Man urged me to do so with his little metal assistant.

"Um, maybe. Who are you guys?"

"We're friends of a friend."

They both laughed.

I didn't get the joke.

"Don't look so worried, Johnny boy," said the driver. "We're just taking a little ride out to the Palm Springs area, that's all."

His English was good, aside from the slight accent, which I couldn't place.

"What's in Palm Springs?" I asked.

My lips felt papery and my tongue was desert dry.

"Sand," said my large captor.

They laughed again. They were regular comedians, these guys. I suppose that was kind of funny, sand. Ha ha, yeah, that was a good one.

I was in no mood for laughing, though. I wondered why they didn't tie me up or blindfold me or anything. I decided it meant they didn't care what I saw because I'd never get the chance to tell anyone about it anyway. Visions of Joe Pesci swinging a baseball bat in the desert played in my mind. I see too many old movies.

"You got a friend there, waiting for you," the driver told me. "He's got a business proposal. An offer you can't refuse."

More laughter.

Maybe they were taking me to a friend. I didn't know, and I was beginning to not really care where I was headed. They got me the fuck away from Patrick — that was a good thing, wasn't it? Anyway, there was no way out of that car, so in my depressingly sober state, I sat back and enjoyed the scenery. Ha, ha, that's a joke, too — there's nothing to look at along the 10 except those big creepy windmills, and they wouldn't come into view for at least another hour.

My cell phone rang. I jumped and locked eyes with the driver in the review mirror.

"Who is that?" he yelled.

"How should I know?" I responded.

Big Man reached into my pocket. I hoped he would stick himself on the hypodermic needle I had in there. He didn't, though. He just jacked my phone and read the display.

"Phone says 'Andy,'" Big Man reported.

It was Patrick. I never listed my contacts' real names, for security reasons. He must have been shitting mad. I secretly enjoyed imagining his panic at my sudden disappearance.

The driver shrugged his eyebrows.

"Turn it off and throw it out the window."

Great. That thing cost me two hundred and fifty bucks and had another hundred dollars' worth of music on it. Bummer.

The rest of the ride was smoke, Jerry Lee Lewis, visions of impending doom, and the occasional random bout of hysterical laughter. The two mobsters sometimes shouted at each other in that crazy foreign language.

I needed a joint. Badly. My hands were starting to shake. Unfortunately, I couldn't fish around in my jacket pockets with Big Man next to me. I thought he'd bust a cap in my ass for sure if I moved. I chewed my nails instead. It was hardly a suitable substitute.

Sometime past dark, we drove straight through Palm Springs and Cathedral City into a small burg called Rancho Mirage. We pulled into a long driveway lined with flood lights and gently swaying palm trees. A Rehabilitation Facility. Gasp. I knew someone in rehab? Maybe it was that fucked up Orange Juice kid. Or were these thugs admitting me? I was confused. I needed to smoke a blunt to clear my head.

Big Man and the driver, neither of whom had yet bothered to introduce themselves to me, escorted me through the luxurious lobby of the sprawling complex. A staff member, stood behind what looked like a hotel check-in desk. She smiled up at us, welcoming us to Rancho Mirage like we were on vacation or something. She picked up the phone and summoned an orderly, or whatever they called them there, to take us to the room she somehow already knew we'd be headed to. Were these fuckers seriously admitting me?

The dimly-lit monochromatic halls were surprisingly quiet. I wondered where the detox patients were puking and screaming and convulsing. Maybe that was only allowed during business hours. Or maybe the rich people who could afford this place didn't do that kind of vulgar stuff. Nah, I was pretty sure detoxing was the great equalizer — everyone pukes and shits themselves just the same. How great is that?

We left the building through an exit at the end of the hall and were led to a row of neat-looking free-standing cottages just past a bottom-lit pool. The miniature buildings reminded me of the shed my grandmother used to have in her backyard, only these were a little bigger and not all rusty and falling down. And I was pretty sure there weren't lawn mowers and gardening junk crammed inside. They were beige, or maybe gray, and each had clean white trim around the roof and the single window. Each little window was sandwiched between dark green shutters, and flowers sprouted from little window boxes below. Kind of nice. Tranquil. I couldn't imagine any puking or screaming going on inside those little playhouses.

The orderly knocked on the forest green door of cabana number eight.

A muffled reply seeped through to my ears: "Yes, come."

My heart stopped.

The orderly smiled and opened the door.

Damien.

DAMIEN

Wednesday, July 14 — Thursday, July 15

I cannot believe this is happening to me.

Twice in my life I've had this same totally fucking surreal sensation. The first time, I stood on a stage in the middle of a stadium filled to capacity with screaming chicks. That totally rocked.

This time, same exact sensation, but totally opposite motivation, you know? I'm watching myself from somewhere above, only instead of it being the most awesome dream known to man, it's bad. Really bad.

I killed somebody.

I fucking *killed* somebody.

Me. *Me*, the super-famous leader of an internationally acclaimed boy band. I know, incredible, right? Fucking out-of-the-stratosphere, unbelievable.

I've been trying to put it out of my mind, but my iPod is letting me down, big time. All I want to do is cry and throw up. And sleep. If I could sleep, that is. I see her face everywhere, that poor, poor girl. I started crying in a coffee shop the other night when a black-haired waitress came to our table to take our order. She didn't look anything like her, except that she had shiny black hair. She's never far from my thoughts, that little girl. I am doing my best to forget, to carry on with my incredibly awesome life, but I'm discovering it may not be possible.

Night time is the worst. I leave the lights on now. I tried turning them off. Once. That first night. She stood in the corner of my room, her sad pale face glowing in the dark, trying me, accusing me, sentencing me. I could hear her gasping for breath, choking, wheezing.

And I screamed.

Sasha snapped on his bedside lamp and backhanded me. I had been screaming at an armoire in his bedroom. The next morning, he checked me into this rehab clinic. I guess I was kind of freaking him out. He said hiding there, in plain sight, was my best option. I trusted him.

When I left home the night that it happened, I went to Sasha. I told him everything. I cried, I begged him to not drop me from the band, I pleaded with him to hide me, to make the whole thing go away.

And I told him that John saw me.

Maybe I should have left that part out.

One thing you have to understand about Sasha is that he put me in this band, and he's taken care of me for the last five years. He's like a second father to me. He heard me sing the Star Spangled Banner at a minor league baseball game when I was sixteen, and he knew that I had talent. He gave me the opportunity of a life time, taking me to Europe and giving me the lead spot in In Dreams.

And you know what? Fuck it. That little whore isn't worth all the shit I've been putting myself through. Star-fucking maggot. Fuck her, man. And fuck John, too. He's gonna suffer.

When Sasha suggested offing my 'friend' John, I mean, it kind of shocked me. It seemed more than a little harsh for this guy who's been so good to me. But I don't know, maybe he's right. I mean, Sasha has never steered me wrong before.

Sasha was a star maker in the Moscow music scene before he came to America and found us. He had put together a couple of bands before, and they were successful, but not worldwide. With us, he wanted to achieve the international stardom that had escaped him before. And we wanted that, too. Who wouldn't? I never thought he was manipulative. That actually didn't occur to me until quite recently.

Anyway, the guy has always been there for me. And right now, I need him more than ever. He's pretty much all I've got. This would absolutely kill my mom if she found out. And she's had a rough enough year, with Daddy dying and all.

I was so completely gutted over what I did that I couldn't function. I felt totally out of control, like I didn't know where I was or what I was doing. Nothing felt real. I don't know if what Sasha wants to do to John is right, but I don't know what else to do.

John. He's a good kid. The week I moved into the loft, I met him out on the steps. I had just come out of the building, and some girl walking by stopped and screamed in my face. She pounced on me and ripped my shirt. It was a little embarrassing. There I was, in front of my new neighborhood with this chick totally wigging out. John was sitting there, drawing and whatever. I asked him for a piece of paper and his pencil. I got the hysterical cat-girl to tell me her name and wrote her an autograph, and she finally left me in peace. I just stood there for a minute, feeling like a god, when I noticed John looking up at me.

"Yeah, I'm him," I said with a glowing grin.

John shook his head and looked away. I thought he was just going to ignore me. I was about to walk away, but he turned and laughed at me, still shaking his head. Jackass. But, he offered me some weed, and we got to talking about music. Before I knew it, I'd kind of made a friend. My first one since before I joined the band. Most people are nice to me because I'm Damien Tungsten, Super Mega-Rich Pop Star, but that's totally different. John didn't care about that. John was genuine. That really did my head in. Fucker didn't respect me, but I taught him.

My stardom was a handicap when it came to dealing with that kid. He was a little distant at first, not knowing what to make of my idol image, put off by seeing me on TV and in the papers. He is kind of a shy kid, never had any friends around or anything, but he warmed up. I think maybe he was a little embarrassed about where he lives and stuff, but I don't give a shit. That's not my problem.

Anyway, I guess I turned out to be okay in his eyes because he hung out with me, smoked pot, and played my guitars most nights when I wasn't out on tour. It was great to have somebody to just shoot the shit with. I really did like the kid.

I feel kind of bad for him. I cried for him as much as I did for myself. *Why the fuck did you have to be looking out the goddamn window, John? Stupid fucker. Now look what you're making me do.*

Sasha says there's only one way to make absolutely sure the kid keeps his mouth shut.

I really wish things could be different. For both of us. But they ain't.

KELLY

WEDNESDAY, JULY 14

As far as I'm concerned, she got exactly what she deserved, the skanky bitch. And I am one hundred percent positive that whatever happened to her, she brought that shit on herself. Damien probably got her out to the car and realized what a total freak she is, and she ran off to some retarded goth club or something, crying her little black heart out. They have those in Hollywood, right, goth clubs? Places where all those lame-ass fake vampires hang out and drink absinthe and talk about how totally unemployed they are? Whatever. The cops probably never even thought to look there. Idiots. They're way more interested in totally destroying poor Damien's career. Fucking cops.

I know, right?

I can only imagine how totally shitty Damien must feel right now. Poor, poor baby. I wonder if I could find him. I know I could comfort him. I could make him feel better. I'm good at that kind of stuff. Like back home, when my history teacher's wife dumped him. Shit, if only that freaking security guard hadn't made me blow him, I would have been the one leaving with Damien that night. He'd like me way better than Scary Mary. Poor boy, he just didn't know any better.

I don't know where he is, but I'm going to find him. I snuck out to Von's and got all the papers that have his picture on the front page. My aunt and uncle's house is busting at the seams with pigs, but do you think a single person even noticed that I had left?

I know, right?

JOHN

Wednesday, July 14 – Thursday, July 15

What the fuck was going on? I felt like I had slipped into some parallel universe or some shit. I was so confused, not to mention scared stiff. What the fuck was Damien doing here? He wasn't an addict. Not then, anyway. The media said he was in rehab, but I thought that was just some kind of cover.

Were these guys going to try to keep me here because I saw what he did? No, that was insane.

But, I knew as soon as I saw the look on Damien's face that they were going to kill me.

I had allowed myself the supreme luxury of a single shred of hope in the car, but that had vanished as soon as I heard his voice through the door. Why bring me to the re-hab hospital? Maybe they knew someone here who would clean up the mess or something. I wondered how they were going to do it. I wondered if everything would just go silent and black. I wondered how badly it would hurt.

Damien sunk deep into a leather club chair, wearing the expression of a scolded six-year-old.

"Hi, John," he said. "How are you?"

His eyes were sunken and dull. His perma-tan had fad-ed to a ghostly pallor. He looked like shit.

"How am I? I'm pissed off, dude. What the fuck are you doing to me, man?"

The best defense is a good offense, or some shit like that, right?

"These assholes almost run me over, then drive me way

out into the fucking desert. Help me out here, Damien, 'cause I'm thinking Goodfellas right about now."

I didn't want to tip my hand and let him to know how scared I was, so I yelled. He looked pretty freaked himself.

"Yeah, um, sorry."

He rubbed the stubble on his chin and looked at the green carpet.

"Listen, I, um... Whew."

He wiped the back of his hand across his forehead.

"I am majorly paranoid about something, okay, and I, um, I just needed to talk to you."

"Why didn't you just hit my cell? You know my number, man."

He didn't need to know about Patrick taking my phone and holding me hostage or any of that shit.

"It had to be in person. I think you know that."

He was somber and quiet. Not his usual effervescent self.

"Well, here I am. Let's have it, dog. You need some smack or something? Your goon over there didn't mention it so, sorry, all my shit's at home," I lied.

"No, no, it's nothing like that. That's my manager, Sasha, by the way."

Sasha waved from the couch.

"He looks like a shady character, and he is, kind of, but he's okay. Sorry if he scared you."

Damien paused and rubbed his eyes.

"Look, I know this is a pretty bizarre situation, but I have to talk to you about what happened at my place on Friday night."

"Friday night?"

I wasn't playing dumb, I just didn't remember what day it was. Time had lost all meaning over the course of the past few days.

"John, I know you saw me. I looked right at you. You looked right at me, man. You saw everything."

He bit his lip. It reminded me of an animal showing its

teeth and, you know, being aggressive.

"I know you did. How many times have you told me about your peeping Tom shit? I always glance up at your window when I walk outside; it's a habit."

My eyes scanned the room, searching for possible exits. Door, window. This place was bigger than it looked from the outside. It had some depth, like a trailer or one of those, what do they call them, shotgun shacks. There were probably other windows, maybe even a back door.

"Listen," Damien said, "I know you saw me, and I can't just let you go running around, knowing that you know everything. You hear what I'm saying?"

He cracked his knuckles.

"I am so sorry. I really wish you hadn't seen. Shit, I wish I had never met her, but bad luck all around."

He smirked.

Out of the corner of my eye, I saw Sasha pull a knife from his pocket. He cleaned his fingernails with its tip. Damien looked at the floor. I could make it to the door, but that guy with the knife would be on me before I could get it open.

Or maybe not.

I bolted and grabbed for the doorknob. In less than a flash, Damien grabbed my arm and twisted it behind my back. Sasha shuffled over, and they helped me to the couch, seating me next to Big Man. Big Man with his little gun.

"Just make it quick and painless, okay?" I tried not to whine. "Please?"

Damien looked annoyed. I could see the wheels creaking to life in his empty pop star head. He searched Sasha's face for something that I couldn't see. An idea visibly struck him. I could almost see the light bulb over his head. Sasha shook his head no, but Damien just smiled and nodded yes. Sasha sighed and rolled his eyes up to the low ceiling.

"I'm not going to waste you!" He laughed like he was watching a funny movie and had just grasped a complex joke. "I mean, Sasha said it was the only way, but I can't do it. Not to you, John."

They had planned to kill me. That was a harsh reality to face, even though I'd suspected it. My stomach flipped.

"Come on, I'm still your friend, man. You're just a kid, and I like you."

He paused for a couple of seconds, studying my eyes.

"I know you wouldn't do anything to hurt me, would you."

It wasn't a question. Then, the light bulb appeared once again. He smiled at me.

It gave me the creeps.

"I've got other plans for you."

PATRICK

Friday, July 16

I didn't know where the fuck that little turd ran off to. I tried calling his cell phone for more than an hour. I couldn't wait around forever. I'd have to find him later. I had a more immediate need to get my shit over to the storage place before more TV people and even more cops showed up. Goddamn it. I never should have let him go anywhere. That's what I get for trusting someone.

In any case, I made some awesome pieces. Works that the entire world will clamor for, works that will ensure my name lives on in infamy, long after I'm gone. She was so easy to work with. A lot like a taxidermy project crossed with what I imagine making pickles would be like.

Once we bled her dry and got the Flotone pumping, she looked a little pinker. That might have been a mistake, now that I think about it. John freaked even harder when she started looking more normal. Anyway, that whole embalming deal was probably unnecessary considering I wound up disassembling her anyway. Oh, well, live and learn, right?

The internal structures, the muscles and organs, were my main focus. Carving them out went pretty smoothly once I got the hang of it. Just like filleting chicken breasts or carving a roast. No biggie. I learned a lot about quite a few new tools and procedures: the use of incision spreaders, nylon bone separators, cavity fluid injectors, tissue dryer and reducer. Oh, and new uses for a cheese grater, garlic press, and pizza wheel. Pretty interesting. I didn't realize how easy it would be to take an eyeball out of the socket with a large melon baller. Sorting out all the junk stuck to the back of it, like the optic nerve and whatever else is in that tangle of shit, is a different story, though. That's worse than trying to trace all the plugs and cords shoved behind your computer desk or entertainment center. But, hey, learn something new every day, right?

I'm sure Damien Hirst would give his left nut to work with that most precious raw material. The whole 'shock and awe' was completely mind blowing. I did my best to savor every second of the experience. Hirst ought to try it sometime. It was total madness. Cross sectioning, slicing, hacking, stapling and suturing. It was almost too much.

And poor John. He missed all the fun.

That little punk.

As soon as I smuggled the majority of my masterpieces down to Santa Monica Boulevard Storage, I came home and flicked on the TV.

And.

There.

He.

Was.

GRETA

Friday, July 16

"

Mrs. Thomas?" The girl's voice floated in broken waves from the glass door to the edge of the parking lot.

Must be the nurse, I thought.

"Just a sec," I answered, taking one last hurried drag off my Salem.

Must be Mom's turn. About damn time — we've been here for almost an hour. I turned and crushed the butt in the hip-high ashtray beside the door. I was surprised to see that the girl waiting for me was not the nurse. She looked too young to be in a dialysis clinic, the poor thing.

"Come quick, it's your son," she said, grabbing my arm.

My son? He wasn't here. He must be on the phone, I thought.

I race-walked toward the reception desk, already reaching for the handset that I didn't see. I hoped he wasn't hurt. Or in jail. Or dead. My heart squeezed into my throat.

"Greta, look!" my mom shouted from the far side of the waiting room, pulling herself up on her walker. "On the TV. It's John!"

Oh, God, what has he done?

I turned my face upward and found the TV screen floating high in the corner. What on earth was that kid doing on TV?

"Somebody, turn it up!" my mom shouted. "That's my grandson!"

She clapped her hands.

"Ssshh," I hissed. "Oh, my God, it is John."

He must have done something really bad. Worse than the time he shoplifted those CDs from Tower Records, and they wouldn't let him go until I came to get him after my shift.

It was a press conference of some kind. KTLA was broadcasting live from the Beverly Hills Hilton. There were reporters and photographers. And there, smack dab at the center of a long table, was my John. He looked so handsome. He was not in handcuffs or even standing next to a cop. Instead of the orange jumpsuit I'd expected, he wore an expensive-looking leather jacket — one I'd never seen before. His hair was nicely combed and... was he wearing make-up? Oh, my gosh. Tears filled my eyes. Our neighbor, that good-looking rock star guy, was smiling next to him, with his arm around John's shoulders.

"... pleasure to announce addition to the In Dreams family."

An older man, who talked funny, put his hand on John's arm and smiled into the camera.

"It is with great pride that I introduce you to Mr. Jake Wolfram."

Applause filled the room, both on TV and right in the doctor's waiting room.

I collapsed. Someone brought me a wax cup filled with cool water.

Jake Wolfram???

JOHN/JAKE

Friday, July 16

Damien and I sat at the center of the dais in a first floor conference room of the Beverly Hills Hilton. A fake wall behind us sported a repeating pattern of the record company logo and the In Dreams insignia. Sasha sat on my left, Damien on my right. The other four band members, all wearing total deer-in-headlights expressions, filled the remaining four folding chairs. The room teemed with reporters, every one of them gawking at me, shouting random questions. I squirmed in my new flash clothes and sipped bottled water as I smiled and kept quiet. I studied every crease on every one of my knuckles with great intensity. I also willed the floor to open up and swallow me. It did not. I sweated.

"Ladies and gentlemen," Sasha spoke into the forest of microphones before us, silencing the crowd. "Hello. Thank you all for coming. I understand we disappeared and left you all in lurch recently and for that, we apologize. However, was not without good reason. Today, it is my pleasure to announce addition to the In Dreams family. It is with great pride that I introduce you to," big breath, "Mr. Jake Wolfram."

I was high on coke, but even without the stimulant, this was fully awesome. They weren't going to kill me! I mean, yeah, I never liked being the center of attention, but this was... different. I was being introduced to Hollywood. No fucking way! Me. John Thomas, from the 'hood.

The name? Yeah, that...

"We have to change name," Sasha told me on the drive back to L.A., smiling in the rearview rectangle.

"What name? My name? You guys know who I am and what I look like."

I was confused. It wasn't like they were putting me in the witness protection program or anything.

"No," Sasha explained, "see, in other countries... To put this delicately, your name, it means..."

He laughed. Big Man and Damien laughed, too. Again, I didn't get the joke.

"John, dude," Damien said, throwing his arm around my shoulders, "in England, your name refers to a certain male body part."

He grinned like a kid caught saying a naughty word. He raised his eyebrows at me. Oh, I got it.

"Oh," I said.

Who knew a John Thomas was a penis? I didn't know any English people, and I'd never been out of the country, so how the fuck was I supposed to know? They said I'd get laughed right off the stage in London and that no one in Europe would take me (or us) seriously. My name was always just kind of there, I guess. I never thought much of it. I didn't think it was that big of a deal, but I didn't really care.

"Well, what should I change it to?"

I guessed Dick Hertz was out.

Sasha came up with Wolfram, which is another name for Tungsten, close to the Russian word for the element he chose for Damien. He had studied to be a chemist in Moscow before worming his way into the music scene, and he had a special fondness for metals. Whatever. Kind of gay being named after Damien, but I liked the sound of Wolfram. It sounded... strong. And Jake, that was my idea. And so, I would become Jake Wolfram, teen idol. Sweet. It wasn't like I had a ton of monogrammed shirts that I'd have to trash or anything.

Anyway, Sasha had arranged the press conference the

night before from the Rancho Mirage cabana. We drove like mad to make it back to town early enough for me to get fitted for some killer threads at a shop on Melrose. Even though I had been totally against having anything to do with a boy band, I had to admit, all the attention and buzz was starting to get to me.

Sitting in that Beverly Hills conference room, in front of all the reporters, Damien smiled at me, and I suddenly felt... good.

"It is with great pride that In Dreams announces the addition of our newest member, an old friend of mine," Damien read out, "Jake Wolfram."

Everyone applauded, and a matrix of flashes dazzled my eyes. I lifted a hand and smiled a little. Embarrassing. I didn't know how the fuck I was going to pull off such an enormous and complicated charade. But, what the hell, it was way better than being buried out in the desert. I tried to enjoy the moment without throwing up. I thought I just might be able to have some fun with this.

I wasn't allowed to answer any questions. Neither was Damien. Sasha handled the whole thing, talking about how I had extensive musical experience, could play the guitar, and had been in the process of auditioning for the group for several months. He also smoothed over Damien's sudden disappearance and super-short stint in the rehab clinic. Piece of cake. The press ate it up and began the process of spinning me into a celebrity. I never knew it was so easy. No sweat.

It was the other guys in the band who were the problem.

JAKE

Friday, July 16

"

What the hell do we need him for?" Reggie, the tough one, demanded, viciously flinging a packet of Splenda across the table at me.

I flinched as it bounced off my chest.

Sasha had called the other band members late last night and asked them to meet us for an early breakfast at the Polo Lounge. He told them it would be followed by a ten o'clock press conference. They knew something was rotten.

Reggie turned to Damien.

"And where the fuck have you been? We're on tour, and you pull a fucking disappearing act? So not cool, bro."

Reggie shook his head and cracked his knuckles. A dignified old lady at the next table shot him such a look over the rim of her tea cup. But she seemed more charmed than frightened by the brooding blond boy in the motorcycle jacket. Reggie was like a cute little kid playing dress-up in a Hell's Angel's closet, then looking to kick some ass at the local playground. He took himself a lot more seriously than anyone else did.

"Chill, Reg," said Sasha.

He had told us in the car that there would be some emotions to deal with.

"Bottom line is, everyone's here, I'm smoothing things over with record company, and life is good. You get right back to tour as soon as new kid catches up on material."

The four guys glared at me like I'd just squeezed out

the loudest, deadliest fart known to man. Damien looked down into his plate of eggs Benedict or whatever the fuck the waiter had set in front of him. Billy, the cute one, Alex, the bad boy, and Scotty, the down-to-earth one, didn't want anything to do with me.

Those guys had been together for about four years or something, had made a name for themselves in Europe, fought long and hard for it, and they resented the hell out of Damien for bringing in a new guy. Especially just out of the blue. Maybe it would have been different if he'd had a reason, like if one of the existing members was always drunk off his ass and was fucking stuff up, but nothing like that had ever happened. Everything had been hunky-dory right up until Damien's... accident. Sasha was the only one who knew about Mary Bellows.

I was seen as an intruder from the second I stepped into that dark wood-paneled dining room. I was not need-ed nor wanted there. The Drab Four, as I would later call them, made that abundantly clear. I felt like jumping out of my hand-carved chair and screaming that it was all Damien's fault and that he killed that chick, and I didn't want any goddamn thing to do with their shitty boy band, anyway. Instead, I bit my tongue and looked at the pool through the wall of smoked glass.

Sasha did his best to sweet-talk the guys, but they were royally pissed. It was all about the money, of course. Well, that and the attention.

"Look at him," Billy whined. "Is he a freaking Lacoste model or what? He's gorgeous," he lisped, raising his hand.

He snapped his fingers and a waiter appeared to take his order for another cosmopolitan. There's no such thing as underage drinking at the Polo Lounge. And it's never too early in the day for a cocktail. Billy studied me and pouted, biting his thick bottom lip.

"Don't worry, man, you'll always be the cute one to me," said Alex, through a mouthful of scrambled eggs.

They all smirked at Billy, the tension breaking. Alex blew Billy a kiss. A chunk of cranberry muffin sailed off his lips, landing in Reggie's orange juice, forcing a reluctant collective laugh from the table.

Damien looked around the table and cleared his throat.

"Listen, you guys, John is a real musician. I really think we could use him. He could teach us some really good stuff, make us believable as a rock act."

He looked at everyone in turn, pleading his case.

"I'm just trying to work on our credibility."

"Credibility? Shit, man, we're a boy band, not a symphony orchestra," said Scotty. "We're not musicians, we're fucking puppets."

He moved his arms up and down, as if they were being pulled by invisible strings attached to his wrists.

"We are a money-making machine for the label, so they can throw money at real musicians who make real records."

He leaned back in his chair and lit up a cigarette. A waiter rushed over with an ashtray and made him put it out.

"Is that all you want to be?" Damien pushed his plate toward the center of the table.

"Don't you want to make real music instead of this bubble gum shit? I thought you did. You guys always said you did. All that time we spent touring around Europe, living in Germany, working like fucking dogs."

Damien looked again into each of his band-mates' faces.

"You guys are full of shit if you say you like what we do, what we are."

No one dared to meet his eyes.

"I'm just trying to take us in a new direction, that's all."

"We just broke the top ten, dude. Here, in America," Alex said, wiping his mouth on the sleeve of his gray thermal shirt. "We can't go messing around with that shit right now, changing our image and all that. What kind of shit are you trying to pull on us? Yeah, man, I hate the shitty music and prancing around like some kind of fairy, too, but it's working, Damien."

Damien looked to Sasha for help. Sasha didn't disappoint him.

"Look, you're halfway through two record deal with label. What do you say we take chance on the kid? Worst happens, you get more publicity out of arrangement."

Sasha held his hands up and looked around.

He had been willing to take the gamble as soon as Damien had put the guitar in my hands the night before. I played Nirvana's 'Polly' on my own in the bathroom of the rehab cabana while he listened at the partly open door. It was kind of like peeing — I was too shy to do it in front of an audience, you know. But my life kind of depended on it, so I did the best I could. And when I came out, that dude looked at me like he'd just found a multi-million dollar winning lottery ticket blowing around the sidewalk. He had actual tears in his eyes, and he hugged me like a long-lost son.

"Teach kid what you do now, let him record new album with you, take him on tour," Sasha counseled. "Then, after you make new deal, maybe he can give you guys new edge, extend life of your careers little bit. You all know this business is fickle bitch, *da*?"

Yeah, no pressure on me, right? I did not see myself as this great musician Damien tried so hard to sell me as. I was a decent guitar player, sure, and no one covered their ears when I sang — on the rare occasion anyone actually heard me. But Christ, I couldn't transform a candy-ass boy band into a real rock group. I don't think anyone could perform that kind of miracle, especially not an inner-city teenage shoe-gazing drug dealer like me. I couldn't stand people looking at me, talking about me. I had to quit giving that boy so much weed — Damien obviously could not handle his shit.

I do have to give Damien credit, though. Instead of offing me in the desert, he did his absolute best to sell me to the band. It was a damn convincing story, too. If it had been a movie or something, I would have fallen for it. By the end of the meal, everyone seemed to feel better about me.

Except for me.

KELLY

Friday, July 16

Who in the hell is this Jake Wolfgram freak? I mean, WTF? Now, *he* looks like Scary Mary's type, the emaciated little punk. His hair is actually yellow. Not blond, but pee yellow. Ugh. And I thought I saw a tattoo on his neck. How disgusting is that? I can't believe he's totally trying to steal Damien's spotlight. He has some fucking nerve.

I know, right?

Damien made In Dreams what it is today. He brought all those guys together and took them to the top. It was no easy road, either, with them having to live over in some third world country and tour for years over in Bulgaria or whatever. I mean, okay, yeah, the kid is kind of hot, but they so don't need him. He's just going to make everything too complicated. What if he's, like, some high-maintenance prima donna or something? He'll make a big scene wherever he goes, whining about, I don't know, not having enough green M&Ms in his dressing room, or raising money for war and peace or something, which will totally get the media all jazzed up. And where will that leave poor Damien? Everyone will just forget all about him if he doesn't get his pictures all over the front pages anymore. How sad would that be?

I know, right?

Somebody has got to do something about this bullshit.

JAKE

Last Two Weeks of July

In the dance studio, the choreographer yelled at me, in German, to watch her feet, not her ass. At least I'm pretty sure that's what she said. She sighed a lot — or maybe gasped — and asked me repeatedly why I could not count to acht (which, someone told me, means eight). Oh, my God, I couldn't take it. I was so freaking clumsy. I did have a sense of rhythm, but somehow it got lost between my brain and my size thirteen feet. Total embarrassment torched my face. It was like being stuck halfway up the rope in gym class, too scared to move, with the whole class laughing at you. Maybe I couldn't handle this whole boy band thing.

"From *zee* top," she spat at me in the wall-length floor-to-ceiling mirror.

I was the only one left dancing, if you could call it that. The other guys went through their moves a couple of times, trying to ignore my pathetic participation, and took a seat to watch the show. It was beyond embarrassing, not to mention intimidating. They still resented me, big time, and I know they were just waiting for me to quit. Oh, if only I'd been afforded that luxury.

Damien sat in a molded plastic chair, off to the side, doing a phone interview while he waited for my sorry ass. That fucker never let me out of his sight. It was like being in jail.

I tripped through a basic jazz square, twirled my arms around my head like a coked up orangutan, and got hopelessly lost somewhere around the fourth step of an unbelievably long and complicated sequence. One thing I had to say about my boy band boys: they could memorize shit like nobody's business. I couldn't figure out how they did it. My guess was their heads were so empty that they had a lot of space up there for that kind of shit.

"*Verdammt*, Jake! Look at *mein feet*. *Wachen*. Watch."

The choreographer's face was bright red, either from exercise or frustration, maybe both. I knew for sure her color did not come from humiliation like mine did. Her feet didn't even seem to touch the glossy maple floor as she blew right through the entire routine in about fourteen seconds. She moved like a Swiss watch. I just stood there, slack-jawed and panting.

She stopped and held up her hands.

"Okay, we are done for today. *Fertig*. You must work on this. It takes practice, practice, practice. Ask any one of these *Jungs*," she gestured to my snickering colleagues. "Get Damien to help you — he can do it."

She picked up her towel and gym bag and marched out. The Drab Four followed her, whispering and laughing. I hated those pricks. They made it all look so easy. I thought there must be something really wrong with me if I couldn't keep up with a pansy-ass boy band.

"Hey, buck up," Damien said from over my shoulder. "You know, I was worse than you at first, but look at me now."

He demonstrated a few smooth disco moves.

Asshole.

"It'll get better."

"I don't want it to get better! This is so fucking gay!"

My voice echoed around the empty studio.

"Don't make me do this in front of millions of people. Please? Come on, have a heart. Kill me now. What do you say?"

That was me, the reluctant and whining pop star. Damien just laughed and led me out the front door. Sometimes I did kind of wish he had just killed me that night in the desert. It was my fondest wish right after dance rehearsals.

The up-side to the whole deal was that I didn't have much time to think about Patrick, or the body, or any of that mess. When I did think about it, though, my insides knotted up, and I got all teary-eyed. I was scared, too. Who knew where Patrick was or what he was thinking? But I tried hard to put him out of my mind and concentrate on the new life I'd been given. I had dance steps to memorize, songs to learn, radio and TV shows to appear on, planes to catch... My schedule was filling up fast.

We were due at Monster Sound Studios in half an hour. I may have been a crap dancer, but voice and guitar were so my things. I'd show those smug bastards. Of course, I wouldn't get to play guitar at live shows, since we had to concentrate on our dancing — gag — but I would be allowed to play on the new album. I was stoked about that. There was my silver lining in this whole pile of shit.

But, shit, come on, a *boy band*???

It was all so fucking hard to swallow. At first, anyway.

Damien seemed to fly under the radar after dragging me into the limelight. He sustained minimal damage to his star image, which I found pretty amazing. Everyone seemed glad to see him come back from his unexplained absence, but, much to his dismay, they seemed a lot more interested in me. I could tell that got under his skin. He was so jealous, even at the beginning.

At first, I found all the attention totally scary. I did not want to tell complete strangers my life story, or pose for their cameras, or listen to all their stupid bullshit. They all wanted to know where I went to school, why my mom and dad got divorced, what I liked to do in my free time. It was only a matter of time before they found out that I'd peddled drugs to nine year-olds and peeped in my neighbors' windows right up until a couple weeks ago. Thank Christ I'd never been arrested.

One kid from the old neighborhood told a reporter that I'd sold him pot a couple of times. The joke was on him, though, because soon after that, the cops came and talked to him about his illegal activity. Everyone else I sold to kept quiet.

The cops came after me anyway.

JAKE

Monday, July 30

"So," good old Grissom — I mean, Detective O'Brien — coughed from across the coffee table. "You know, we've been trying to catch up with you."

He squinted at Damien, who lounged comfortably on the velvet sofa next to me.

Damien was totally cool. Not a bead of sweat or a strand of hair out of place.

Sasha had rented us this suite at a famous Hollywood hotel, the one where that fat old comedian OD'ed a long time ago. Damien thought he had to keep me under lock and key, and we couldn't go back to the old neighborhood for obvious reasons. So the hotel became our new home. After a couple of days of rock star living, the living room of our suite looked like a total dump. There were dirty dishes covered in half-eaten food and cigarette butts in the sink, on the counters, on the coffee table, everywhere. Ketchup-stained linen napkins, smelly sweat-socks and cast off T-shirts lay strewn across the floor in heaps. And the place probably didn't smell very good, either.

It was a shame that old Grissom found us. Damien was okay, though. Confident, even. He knew the cops were working over his apartment, but I didn't think he was ready to talk to them yet. He seemed fine, the sly prick.

Damien cleared his throat and smiled politely at the officer.

"Sorry. I haven't been well," he said.

"I heard that."

The cop gazed around our own private landfill, looking at the heaps of entertainment trades and sheet music on the table in front of him. His gaze fell on a brand new is-sue of *Rolling Stone* magazine graced with Damien's ugly mug.

I sweated through my new vintage Richard Hell T-shirt and downed half of a Red Bull. I resisted the urge to jump up and down on the coffee table. I wished I hadn't taken that ecstasy. As if he'd read my thoughts, the cop's eyes tracked to my face. I wiped my mouth on the back of my hand, hiding a smile. I was glad that I had my shades on; at least he couldn't see my enlarged pupils.

"And, you, Mr. Thomas — *Wolfram*, I mean — it's nice to see you again."

He smiled at me with all the warmth of a rattlesnake.

"I seem to recall asking you not to go anywhere. Re-member, when we talked at your apartment?"

How could I forget my memorable Oscar-losing perfor-mance of 'Dances with Diarrhea?'

"Um, yeah, well," I tried to convey an air of arrogant detachment. "I am still in L.A. County."

I think it came across as nervous confusion. Damn. Why did he always show up when I was wasted?

"So, I didn't really go anywhere."

Grissom pursed his lips. I resented him questioning me. Again. I knew I should have been scared out of my mind, but I was high on Planet Rock Star. My ego had grown way out of control in just a few short days.

"Part of the band now, I see," he said.

I didn't respond. I tapped my foot to the rhythm of a song that played in my head. He looked like he wanted to smack me. I wasn't in the mood to feel intimidated. I tried on my new rock star smirk. It felt pretty good.

Damien appeared even less vulnerable. He studied the textured carpet, his forehead creased in concentration as he picked up a newspaper. As if hoping for an easier target, Grissom swung his attention back to him.

"And, Mr. Cole — or should I say Tungsten?" He grinned like a shark. "We have completed our search of your apartment. It's all clear, and you may return to it any time you wish."

Grissom raised his caterpillar eyebrows at Damien's audible sigh.

"I'm sure you'll be relieved to know that no evidence of involvement in Ms. Bellows' disappearance was discovered."

Damien's lips curled at the corners. He inhaled deeply and raised his shoulders.

O'Brien narrowed his eyes, keeping them on Damien's.

"In fact, we ended our search early, when incriminating evidence was found in Mr. Salinger's residence, down the hall."

Old Grissom's eyes jumped to me. Past his shoulder, an arm floated out from behind the curtain; Mary's arm; the one I watched Patrick saw off. The muscles around my mouth tightened involuntarily. The arm vanished. Whoa. I lit a cigarette, fumbling it a bit, and put my feet up on top of a stack of magazines, which went cascading down the opposite side of the table. I put my feet down and coughed.

"Mr. Salinger is now the sole suspect in the case," Grissom said in my direction.

He didn't sound like he was on board with that. I took a deep drag on my cigarette and blew smoke rings at the ceiling, regaining my cool. Holy shit.

"You know, Mr. Tungsten," O'Brien shot back to Damien, "a witness does place the victim in your company on the night of her disappearance."

Damien's smile hardened. A door slammed shut somewhere behind his eyes.

The detective searched the fortress of his face.

"Unfortunately, she doesn't seem very reliable."

I swallowed hard and looked out the window, picturing that girl from the Bellows' press conference, mouthing that ominous threat. I looked for the arm in the curtains, but it was gone. I was losing my shit.

So, we were off the hook. Or O'Brien wanted us to think we were, anyway. Maybe I was just being paranoid.

O'Brien stood to go. He paused at the door and turned to me.

"Mr. Thomas, you wouldn't happen to know where Mr. Salinger is these days, would you?"

PATRICK

Sometime, Last Two Weeks of July

"

I don't expect you to understand. I just have to... go away for a while."

My mom didn't answer. I didn't know if she'd hung up the phone or if she was just giving me the silent treatment. Almost a minute passed before she spoke.

"Well, what about your exhibition? We were all so excited about that. What happened there?"

I sighed. How could I possibly explain this situation to my mother?

"Listen, I can't talk right now. Just... I gotta go."

I hung up and stepped onto the subway. Maybe I'd hang at the beach for a while. I brought my skateboard and a backpack with some clothes and toiletries.

Everyone on the train stared at me.

But I hadn't been on TV yet.

DETECTIVE O'BRIEN, L.A.P.D

(aka, GRISSOM)

Last Two Weeks of July

"Hey, Detective."

Officer Rodriguez pulled me away from Damien Tungsten's refrigerator. Fresh produce, milk more than a week away from its expiration date, pizza box with a receipt dated four days ago. The guy's obviously been here in the last few days. The Chinese take-out didn't smell that fresh, but who could tell from that garbage?

"What?" I threw the stainless steel door shut.

"You, um, you smell anything walking past that other apartment?" Rodriguez asked, glancing around at the concert tour posters hanging in frames along the wall.

He was pretty good for a rookie, but he was a little short in the confidence department.

"No," I sniffled. "Can't smell a thing with this frigging cold. Why?"

"Coming off the elevator, I thought I smelled something," he said, "like, some chemical smell, you know? I don't know what it could be, and it might not have anything to do with this case, but you know, maybe we should check it out?"

Asking, not telling.

"Yeah? Well, we gotta question the neighbor anyway, so why don't you take Phillips over there," I pointed to another uniformed kid who was working the case, "and check it out."

"Okay, you got it Detective," he chirped.

I thought he was going to salute me for a second. Rookies.

Detective Collins approached me, phone pressed to his ear.

"We have confirmation that Damien Tungsten has checked into a rehab facility out in Rancho Mirage."

Okay, that was one question answered. We were close to clearing his apartment. There was nothing conclusive linking him to the victim. Shit.

Yesterday, down at my office, a little girl — Mary's cousin, told me a story.

Her aunt and uncle brought her into the interrogation room and sat her down across the table from me. Her aunt patted her shoulder, and they stepped out, leaving us alone.

I smiled at her, trying to put her at ease, even offered her a soda. She gave me that smug teenager attitude, the one that makes you want to smack them one.

"Kelly," I said, "I'm Detective O'Brien."

I waited for a 'how do you do,' or even just a 'hi,' but she just glanced at me, smacking her gum.

"I hear you went to the In Dreams concert the other night."

"Uh-huh."

She twirled her hair and looked at herself in the two-way mirror.

"Mary went with you, is that right?"

"Yeah."

"Was anyone else with you?"

She coughed. "No."

"Did she go home with you afterwards?"

"Uh-uh."

Her gum snapped, echoing. Was she trying to hide something? I thought it was possible, but I couldn't determine any probable motivation. From what Mr. and Mrs. Bellows said, Kelly and Mary were the best of friends.

"When is the last time you saw your cousin?"

"Um, before the show."

"Was she inside the auditorium?"

"Yeah."

"Were you in your seats?"

"No."

"Can you tell me where you last saw her?"

She didn't answer.

"Kelly? Tell me where you last saw her, please," I said, trying not to raise my voice.

Teenagers aggravated the hell out of me.

She looked annoyed. "At the Palladium."

"Kelly, you know, dear," my voice grew a touch sarcastic, "your cousin could be lost right now, laying in a ditch with her legs broken, or maybe in some sick psycho's basement somewhere, fighting for her goddamn life with her arms tied and a gag in her mouth."

I slammed my hand on the desk for emphasis.

She was unmoved.

"Now, damn it, tell me where you last saw her."

She sighed and looked at me like she was bored to death.

"Okay. The green room, you know, backstage."

Right.

"Was that before or after the show?"

It didn't matter which she chose, I knew she was bullshitting me. I tried not to roll my eyes, which would only stop her from talking at all.

"I don't know."

Liar.

"Yes, you do."

I was tired of her. This was pointless.

"Okay, um, it was... after."

She snapped her gum again.

"Just a second ago, you said you last saw her before the show."

I watched her blink her eyes, uncross and recross her legs.

"Now, I want you to think really hard, Kelly. Was it before or after the show? And who did you see her with?"

She stared into my eyes. Hers were artificially blue, probably colored contact lenses. A small scar, less than one inch in length, curved upward from the crooked bridge of her nose. Nose broken in a childhood accident or some sort of domestic abuse situation. Her body language indicated an unwillingness to divulge information.

"Damien Tungsten," she finally hissed through gritted teeth.

Of course, I didn't buy it, but it was all we would get from her.

So I sent a unit to search Mr. Tungsten's apartment and had them take apart the bed, the closets, the kitchen, the bathroom, and whatever else was there. Not surprisingly, the investigation didn't turn up a damn thing.

I stood in that apartment wondering what that girl's cousin could be hiding.

Rodriguez and Phillips went to knock on the neighbor's door. No answer. I told them to keep an eye on the place and try again later. After the neighbor didn't show up for two days, we called the landlord. I didn't expect to find anything, but I had the guy open the door for us anyway.

Holy Jesus, Mary, and Joseph.

To say that we were unprepared for what greeted us in Apartment Number Four would be a gross understatement.

Flies buzzed around a small mound of what appeared to be discarded human skin in the middle of a plastic sheet spread across the living room floor. A rusty and paint-splattered bucket, filled three-quarters of the way with blood, sat in a corner. A paint brush floated in the thick stinking liquid. Someone had painted the large plasma television screen red. The word 'ME,' also in red, stretched across one spacious concrete wall, almost floor-to-ceiling. There were three gigantic and frightening paintings, or collages, of some sort, featuring a Frankenstein-like face.

I didn't know if all of the strange objects we found were related to a crime, but even if they weren't, this guy was some kind of psycho. At first, we didn't know if the place was a crime scene or not.

But, then, Rodriguez found it.

One dog collar, black leather, approximately nineteen inches in length, one inch wide. Rabies tag, attached, issued by Orange County, California, current year. Item found located on a south-facing kitchen counter in the apartment belonging to one Patrick Salinger, thirty-four, self-employed artist. Salinger is a party of interest and remains at large.

JAKE

Tuesday, July 31 —

Wednesday, August 1

The house jutted out of the hill halfway up Laurel Canyon. Damien put his window down and pressed the button on a little black box, which sat on top of a post anchored in a pile of large rocks. The wide wrought-iron gate swung open, bidding us a silent welcome. Billy's petite sapphire Miata clung to the garage end of the steep driveway, next to Alex's full-sized Hummer. I felt like throwing up. Here I was, hanging with the stars.

The guys in the band hadn't been very friendly since I'd shown up, but stuff was starting to turn around. Silly me — I thought it was, anyway. After a week of totally blowing me off, and then realizing that I wasn't going anywhere, they'd invited me over to hang at the house, shoot some pool, play video games or whatever. I was actually pretty psyched.

Damien was unusually quiet on the ride over from the hotel. I asked him what was up, and he just said he had a headache. I smoked a cigarette and wondered, star struck and daydreaming, what the house would be like. God, what was wrong with me? I should have known something was rotten from the way Damien had been acting.

The Drab Four — Billy, Alex, Reggie, and Scotty — all lived in this house hidden away in the Hollywood Hills. The record company encouraged this cost-saving arrangement from the beginning when the guys were teenagers and living in Europe. It had become natural for them, but I wondered if it drove them a little crazy sometimes. They were always together. I didn't know if I could handle that. I liked my space.

The house itself looked like a couple of squashed cracker boxes stuck together, forgotten amongst the trees and rocks. I had always imagined houses in Hollywood as huge mansions, three- story stone monstrosities with huge-ass columns flanking the front door. This looked more like a small-scale city parking garage. But instead of cars parked on the roof, it had a pool.

Damien and I walked right in. It wasn't locked or anything. And since the rent was paid out of the band's recoupable expenses, Damien felt a rightful sense of ownership, so he strolled right in. I crept along behind him as he strolled past the thoroughly modern kitchen and straight into the 1970s. The family room, where all the guys were shooting pool and listening to Michael Bolton, was half alive with orange shag carpeting, dark wood paneling, and white melamine space furniture. As sickened as I was by the interior decorating, the view was absolutely supreme. The entire city of Los Angeles spread out beneath us, a fucking gigantic grid of miniature twinkling lights stretching farther than I'd ever seen in my life. I stumbled directly to the window and drooled.

There was some whooping and hollering that passed for some sort of greeting. I turned from the window and saw Damien shaking everyone's hand with their secret handshake or whatever. They all whispered and giggled together like a bunch of high school bitches, casting glances at me between snickers. Yeah, hi.

Reggie walked up to me and put a cold bottle of beer in my hand, then led me over to the rest of the group at the pool table. They all seemed to be in pretty good spirits, but I couldn't help feeling a little suspicious. I thought this was supposed to be a friendly visit, you know, but something just didn't feel right.

"Well, what do you think? You like the view, huh?"

Reggie slung his arm around me like we'd been best buds for years.

"Welcome to Paradise."

"Thanks," I said.

I downed my beer in a single gulp. The gesture was cheered, and another beverage magically appeared in its place.

By the time the guys finished playing pool, I'd had five beers and was feeling better. That outsider feeling I'd had when we showed up had melted away as the beer flowed, and the guys started telling me road stories. I actually started to feel like part of the group. It was kind of nice.

"Hey, new kid, since you haven't asked why Damien doesn't live here," Scotty said, chalking his pool cue, "I'll fill you in on that situation."

Damien looked at the floor, embarrassed. He seemed distracted, like he'd rather be anywhere else at that moment. I would soon find out why.

"He's too good for the communal living shit," Scotty said, lining up his shot, "now that we're back in the states. As our 'leader,' he has to project an image of maturity."

Scotty stood up and let out a floor-shaking belch. Everyone laughed. Except for Damien.

The guys put their cues back in the rack and formed a loose circle around me. At first I thought they were going to sing a song.

"Hey, you know what song I'm really digging," I asked, smiling like a retard. "I'm really liking 'Hey, Bling Tang.'"

It was going to be the first single from our new album. I was such a complete idiot.

It finally dawned on me. They were sizing me up. Like a pack of hyenas around a... whatever it is hyenas fucking hunt down and kill. Billy came up behind my left shoulder and blew in my ear. His breath stunk. Alex stepped up on my right, Scotty next to him. Reggie pulled Damien over to stand next to Billy. They all wore smiles, but something had changed in their eyes, in the set of their mouths. They glanced at each other, exchanging some kind of silent signal. It definitely felt like trouble. The thought of bolting from the house fleetingly touched my mind.

"So, Damien," said Billy, "when is our new roommate moving in?"

He looked at me and made a kissy gesture that freaked me the fuck out. I looked down and noticed the ginormous sapphire ring glittering on his dainty hand.

"Yeah, buddy," said Alex, "we want to make our new brother feel welcome."

Alex thrust his hand out and gave me a less than welcoming shove.

"This is a friendly little group we've got here."

I stumbled backward, confused. This did not feel friendly to me. I couldn't figure out what had happened in the last minute or two. Where did the love go?

Someone pushed me from behind. I stumbled into Billy. I felt his hot breath on my cheek, his hand on my back.

"We're just like family," Billy said, right before he slammed his fist into my stomach.

I felt that sapphire ring rip my shirt and make a trench in my gut. I doubled over with laughter tickling my ears. I stood up and was about to ask what that was for when someone else landed a punch just above my left kidney. Tears flooded my eyes, but there was no way I was going to cry in front of those fuckers.

Damien finally spoke up.

"Guys, not the face, we've got a photo shoot coming up."

That's all he said. Why didn't he do something to help me? What the fuck?

I was knocked off balance by a kick that glanced off my hip bone. I fell on the floor and Reggie straddled me, kneeling on my forearms, his sharp kneecaps pinning me to the floor. He punched me in the chest and shoulders until he was out of breath, and I hacked up a huge wad of bloody phlegm. Reggie grabbed me by the jacket and pulled me to my feet. Scotty landed a roundhouse kick on my thigh, then he grabbed Damien by the arm and brought him over to me. We stood there, face to face, looking into each other's eyes. His were empty.

Scotty said, "Go, Damien, you pussy," giving him a nudge.

And Damien booted me square in the nuts.

I didn't cry. No matter how hard they punched or how many times they kicked, I would not give them the satisfaction. It was so fucked up, the whole situation. I imagined it was like being the new guy on the high school football team. At least I didn't get my ass cheeks taped together.

Damien. He didn't say a goddamned word the whole time they were beating the shit out of me. He just wore his 'mature' expression and then thumped me just as hard as the rest of them. That prick. After all the shit that I did for that bastard, he let those fucking assholes kick my ass. And he helped them. *Betrayal* was the word that filled the space of my mind. I had never known its true meaning until that night.

We rode back to the hotel in silence. I stole a couple of sideways glances at Damien. He kept his empty eyes bolted to the road.

Back within the safety of my hotel room, I crawled into bed without bothering to take off my clothes or shoes. I spat blood on the carpet and consulted the dwindling stash of painkillers in the top drawer of my nightstand. I dry swallowed some Oxycodone and shut my eyes. I could feel the bleeding beneath my skin, bruises swimming to the surface, fire in my side where Billy's ring had cut me.

I lay in the dark, on my king-sized bed, weighing my options. I could go to the cops.

Bzzzzzzzzz. Aw, thanks for playing, but that's not the answer we were going for.

I could bust out of here and go home to my mom.

Bzzzzzzz. Survey says: keep your mouth shut!

Keep your mouth shut *is* the correct answer.

Through the game show soundtrack in my head, I became aware of someone tapping on my door. It opened a crack, like my eyes, and I saw Damien thrust his head in. His face was a blank canvas.

I shut my eyes, not caring whether his intention was to kick me in the nuts again or to apologize. I was too worn out to give a shit. He was not my friend.

Damien strode in and sat at the foot of my bed. He cleared his throat about seven times during the long silence that spilled out between us.

"John, I know you won't believe me, and I can't say I blame you," he said, "but I'm sorry."

His theatrical sigh shook the bed.

"You have to understand that those guys have been through hell and back together. They see you as some hot shot kid looking for an easy ride. They wanted you to pay your dues, that's all. A little hazing — you can handle that."

He laughed a little.

I didn't.

"Look, I know it's my fault that you're in this mess, John, but I can't tell them. I can't ever tell them the truth. I *can't*. All of their careers would be over. Do you understand that, man? They'd become another boy band joke. They'd be devastated. Just because I made one fucking stupid mistake. What the fuck am I supposed to do?"

I didn't give a shit what he did as long as it didn't include me. I would never forgive him for any of this, not for stealing my life, not for holding me hostage, and not for letting those faggots kick my ass. Fuck him.

Then, like the glimmer of a sapphire ring, a new thought. A plan. Yes, a brilliant plan, unfurling somewhere in the depths of my midbrain. Something in me had snapped. A bright light suddenly flicked on. Or maybe off.

My lips disappeared in a grimace as I lurched into a semi-upright position. I looked at Damien's disgusting sneering face.

And I smiled.

"It's okay, man," I croaked. "I understand. You've got a lot of people depending on you, a lot of fucking responsibility."

I soothed him, lulled him into a false sense of security. I'd show him what betrayal was.

He looked down at the scrapes on his knuckles that came from punching me in the mouth.

"What were you supposed to do?" I murmured. "Listen, open my top drawer there, would you? I know you're in pain, too. I can help you. I'm here for you, man."

He stared into my eyes, and he gave me a blinding Botox smile. His eyes widened when he saw the pill bottles heaped in my nightstand.

"Take two out of the last bottle on the right, okay? 'Take two tablets and call me in the morning.'" I even managed a weak laugh, ha, ha, until the fireball in my left side seared a hole in my world.

Damien shook out the pills, muttered his thanks, and promised that we'd talk in the morning. I slept like a baby for the first time since he killed that bitch.

JAKE

Wednesday, August 1 —

Wednesday, August 15

I got up early the next morning and opened the door for the room service guy. He brought the usual scrambled eggs, bagels, orange juice, and Coke. I fell down on the couch in the suite's small living room, mindful not to touch my left side on anything I could avoid since it was majorly sore from my night of hazing, and I lit up a smoke. A hot knife punched a hole in me, and I coughed, which hurt so much more. I wondered how long it took to recover from getting your ass kicked. I'd never really been in a fight before, but I broke a rib once, falling down some stairs, and it felt pretty similar. I'm sure the guys had broken at least one, probably more, of my ribs the night before. Great, dance rehearsals would be even more torturous, and not just because I couldn't count to *acht*.

I sat watching ribbons of smoke curl off the cherry tip of my cigarette, listening for any sign of life in the suite. I tiptoed over to Damien's door and pressed my ear against it. I didn't hear a sound through the heavy wood. No TV or running water or anything. All was quiet.

I lurched as quickly as I could over to the breakfast cart, keeping one eye on Damien's door. From my jeans pocket, I extracted one very small Ziploc baggie. From the baggie, I extracted about a quarter to a half teaspoon of white powder and stirred it into one of the glasses of orange juice. A knock on the suite's front door made me drop my spoon, lighting another flare in my side.

I hobbled over to the door and peered through the peep hole. It was Sasha. No doubt there to pick us up for rehearsal. He was a little early, but that was his M.O. I pulled the door open.

"Hey, Sasha," I said. "Come on in. I was just watching some TV, trying to wake up. Damien's still in his room. You want a bagel or anything?"

"Thanks, kid," Sasha said, "but I brought my own breakfast."

He held up a paper coffee cup from a trendy shop down the street. He eyed me up and down, squinting at my face. I realized that he knew those assholes beat me up. Dickhead. He crossed the room, sat on the couch, and grabbed the *USA Today* off the coffee table. I willed the ceiling to fall on his fat greasy head, but it didn't.

I grabbed the non-fucked-with glass of O.J. from the breakfast tray and headed to my room.

"I'm going to hit the shower. Back in a few."

In my bathroom, I struggled to pull my shirt over my head. The inside of the hem dragged up the left side of my ribcage like barbed wire. I broke out in a sweat. I looked in the mirror and regarded the source of my agony. My whole side was covered in dark purple blooms edged in various shades of pink and red. A three-inch gash from Billy's ring furrowed down the center of the bruise, just beginning to scab over.

The shower's spray hit me like fistfuls of nails. I side-stepped the deluge and washed my hair with just my right hand since lifting my left anywhere near my head made me wince. Having rinsed out most of the shampoo/conditioner, I shut off the water and toweled myself dry. I kept my eyes on the floor, so I wouldn't see that ugly bruise in the mirror. I got dressed, swallowed a couple of Vicodans, and went back out to the sitting room.

"Good morning, bro," Damien mumbled, spraying the coffee table with tiny shards of egg.

He was pretty gross sometimes, like, you know, a regular guy. The orange juice glass in front of him stood empty. I felt a mad scientist chuckle rise in my throat, but I choked it off.

"'Sup, man? How are you feeling?"

He was pretty chipper (if I may borrow a word from my grandma). I stepped over to the coffee maker and poured a cup. Normally, I don't drink the stuff, but Damien makes a full pot every morning. It smells good, but it tastes like ass. I wonder if it all tastes like that, or if Damien just makes shitty coffee.

"I'm tip-top, mofo, ready to get to work," he said with cheer.

I was surprised to see that he'd eaten his entire breakfast. His appetite had not been that great since we'd moved into the hotel. I smiled to myself.

The morning grind continued, and we started our day with Damien totally on a tear.

"John, oh, my God," he wailed at me in the back of the car, on the way to the studio. "We only have a few months to get you show-ready! Sasha, how many days do we have?"

Sasha stared blankly at Damien's animated visage. I was sure that he was accustomed to the old, stoic, in-control Damien and had just been getting used to the post-murdering, even-more-stoic, Damien when this new manic Damien surfaced. The confusion showed on the Russian's clean-shaven face.

By the time Sasha was about to speak in answer to Damien's question, he had already sped along to another topic of conversation.

"Oooh, look, Pink's! Let's do hot dogs for lunch!"

He actually clapped his hands, like a little kid. Then his voice took on a conspiratorial tone.

"But don't tell Billy. Have you noticed how much weight he's gained in the last month?"

He clicked his tongue and looked out the window. I silently speculated that Damien would not be hungry at lunch time.

He prattled on and on about some book he was reading about the government or something stupid like that. He couldn't seem to shut up. It was like someone had flipped a switch.

Or doped him up.

Heh heh heh. I felt that mad scientist chuckle threatening to surface again as we sailed down Wilshire and stopped in front of the invisible mirror-clad building that housed our recording studio.

I was relieved that we'd arrived before my head exploded. I reminded myself to never forget my iPod again. Damien's mouth was totally out of control. I wondered how his mind was processing such random stuff at that breakneck speed. Then I remembered the few frenzied days I'd spent in the grip of the crack pipe. For me, it had been like being stuck on the Tilt-a-Whirl. Dizzying and nauseating. I pondered ways to keep him high but quiet at the same time. Hmm... Barbiturates? Good old-fashioned Valium? Those didn't sound like they'd be as much fun as coke or meth. I wanted a show.

Inside the studio, Damien continued his machine gun monologue. He ran from the mixing board in the control room to the mic in the sound booth.

"Damn it, Alex, you're too loud," he bitched. "All I'm hearing in my headset is fucking feedback."

He yelled at everyone to look out as he rushed around.

"Where's Jane?" Damien's personal assistant/flunkie. "Jane!" he yelled out into the hallway.

She hurried in and stood by the mixing board, pushing up her horn-rimmed glasses and smoothing down her dyed jet black hair.

"I want sushi. Now. And none of that fucking fake crab shit in the California roll. Chop, chop!"

He faked a lunge at her, and she ran out of the room with a squeak.

Harsh, huh?

He was throwing around four-letter words, yelling at

everybody. Actually, he sounded like a real rock star for the first time since I'd met him. I'd never seen him at work, I guess. But I'm sure a little chemical assistance had him amped up.

Over the course of the next couple of weeks, I stirred gradually increasing amounts of the white powder into his food (at the beginning) and drinks (more frequently, since his appetite disappeared). It worked beautifully. By the end of two weeks, Damien was a certifiable junkie.

And he needed me more than ever. *Who's your daddy?*

Damien would wake up in the morning and appear in the living room of the hotel suite looking like he'd just crawled out of a crypt somewhere. He sweated when it was cold, shivered when it was hot. He talked a mile a minute and moved with lightning speed when he was up; he sat on the floor, propped up by the wall or the bottom edge of the couch, complaining of aches and pains when he was down.

"John, I feel like shit," he croaked as I waltzed out of the kitchenette holding a big glass of Coke.

"Aw, here, drink this, bud." I bent down to hand him the glass, smiling inwardly at the red rims of his bloodshot eyes and the smell of vomit on his morning breath. "You'll feel better soon."

"I feel hungover, man, and I didn't even drink last night," he said between gulps.

"Maybe you have the flu or some shit."

"Yeah, maybe. I haven't had that since I was a kid. I don't remember it feeling like this, though. Sometimes, I feel great, you know, better than I've ever felt in my life. But, then..." His voice trailed off, and his shoulders seemed to slump even further at his sides.

Commercials blared from the TV telling us that: 1) we might have to dress up like pirates if we didn't check our credit reports; 2) we should call the doctor if we have an erection that lasts more than four hours, and 3) we need to pay a crew of thousands to follow us around in case our cell phones need service.

Damien sat up and stretched his long monkey arms toward the ceiling, emitting a long grunt. He grinned at me.

"I think I am starting to feel better. Thanks for the Coke, man."

He paused for a second.

"Hey, John, I've been meaning to ask you about something."

He looked at the floor and cleared his throat.

"I'm kind of curious about something. You, um... you use a needle sometimes, right?"

Ah, I'd been waiting for this moment! Sweet!

"You, um... you think you could show me how?"

A slow smile spread across my face. No problem, I thought.

No problem whatsoever.

KELLY

Wednesday, August 15 —

Thursday, September 20

So, I, like, found out that In Dreams is recording a new album. Yay, right? But, wait, that's not the good part. I found out where they're recording it. Yeah. So, seeing that I'm stuck here while the big investigation is going on, and I have all the time in the world since the cops all think I'm full of shit, I scammed my aunt's car a couple of times and drove to L.A. to this big fancy mirrored building on, I think, Wilshire? Hoping to, you know, see Damien. And maybe that piece of shit, Jake Wolfie or whatever. Anyway, the first two times I went, I hung around from morning 'til night, and I didn't see a freaking thing. I got a lot of weird looks from people, but, what, they've never seen anyone being discreet before? (Okay, I was hiding in the bushes, but they didn't know I had a knife or anything. Jeez.)

The third time, I got lucky.

It was early in the morning, like, maybe seven or something. Traffic kind of sucked, but I cranked some Vampire Weekend in the car, and it wasn't that bad. Anyway, I got to the place on Wilshire or wherever, parked the car, and headed for my favorite hedges. Well, you can imagine how surprised I was to find this crusty old hobo in my spot.

"Excuse me," I said to the guy, "but, I kind of need to wait for somebody here. Would you mind, like, moving or something?"

He had been tying his shoe, so he stood up and was all like, "Well, I'm waiting for someone, too, and I don't know how long they're going to be. You're welcome to wait with me, if you'd like."

I know, right?

Well, he made me a little bit nervous, but he was kind of cute, in a deranged bum kind of way. I didn't really want to hang with him, so I figured I'd move down to another hedge, on the other side of the bus stop. The view of the recording studio's front door wasn't as good, but you could still see from there, I guess.

Just as I started to, like, walk away, the guy says, "Hey, do I know you? You look familiar."

And, I was thinking, like, *'Oh, Christ, not this bullshit come-on line,'* but, like I said, he was kind of cute, so I bit.

"Um, no, I don't think so," I said. "I do get that a lot, though."

I did kind of look like Britney before she, you know, had kids. The guy flicked his head to clear his bangs out of his eyes and stared at me. He had the weirdest silver eyes. Kind of cool, but weird. And — this was totally bizarre — he was holding a dog collar in his hands. One that looked *tres* familiar.

"So, who are you waiting for?" he asked with a smile.

I didn't say anything because I was too busy silently freaking out over the dog collar. It was Mary's.

"I'm waiting for this friend of mine," he went on, since I didn't speak. "I thought he was a good kid, you know, but, I don't know, something happened, and I don't think he's my friend anymore."

I just looked at the guy. I had no idea what to say or do. I thought maybe I should run, but he grabbed my arm before I had a chance.

JAKE

Wednesday, August 15 —

Thursday, September 20

The legalities of adding me as a new band member, mid-contract, proved to be a little sticky. In Dreams had signed a two record firm deal with Serendipity Records way before I came along. The band's recoupable debt was astronomical, but I'll get to that in a minute. I thought I was going to be a super-rich rock star, but Damien set me straight as I sat in the dentist's chair getting cleaned, Zoomed, and Invisaligned.

"Of course, you can make a shitload of bank," Damien said from his seat on the floor next to the dentist's stool. "It just takes a lot of luck."

My reply was limited to "uh-huh" or "unh-unh," punctuated by the occasional lilting "nnn?" or more plaintive "ow." I hadn't been to the dentist since I was about ten. The experience had not become any more fun since then. If anything, it was much worse — the antiseptic smell brought me right back to Patrick's loft. I shuddered and tried to concentrate on Damien.

"See, the way things are set up, most rock stars are fucking drowning in debt. Yeah, they may have the mansions and the cars and all that, but..."

"Spit, please," the dentist directed me.

He seemed okay with patients bringing an entourage along to their appointments. Mine consisted of Damien and Sasha. Sasha spent the whole time in the hall, though, shouting obscenities into his phone. I struggled to sit up, almost passing out from the sharp stab in my side. I spat in the sink and wiped my mouth on the waffle paper clipped around my neck. I tasted blood.

"... they don't own half that shit. Sure, if you're super-popular," Damien continued, absently turning the pages of *The Hollywood Reporter*, "like U2 or Lady Gaga, you can recoup your expenses, no problem, with plenty of coin left over. Get it?"

My mouth hurt, my side hurt, and a Vicodan fuzz clouded my mind. I had no freaking idea what he was blathering about. But I wasn't clueless for long. The complexities were better explained an hour or so later at the meeting we had with the record company. I got schooled.

Sasha and I sat with the rest of the band and my mother at a huge-ass table in the label's conference room. The furniture was all black leather and chrome but not in a cheap retro way, matching the platinum albums that shone from the walls like silver moons in a night sky. My teeth ached, encased in their new plastic straightening appliances. I couldn't seem to swallow enough. I tried my best not to drool in my lap. I wanted a beer, but I didn't have the balls to walk over to the wet bar and grab one in front of grown-ups, so I just sat there, drooling and hurting.

Since Serendipity Records was the winner of a bidding war in their quest to sign In Dreams, the band had a little clout, but not much. Sasha, who turned out to actually know what he was doing, got me added to the contract after some posturing and empty threats, but the band didn't get any more money out of the deal.

"Mr. Jeffrey Cole," explained one of the suits, "has agreed, for some unknown reason," he shot Damien a quizzical look, "to split his portion of all mechanical and performance royalties with Mr. Thomas."

Everyone looked at Damien like they were waiting for an explanation. He didn't give one.

"Mr. Cole, please sign here."

The lawyer pushed a short stack of papers under

Damien's nose.

I made a startling sucking sound and everyone glared at me.

"Thorry," I said.

I wanted to hide under the table, where I could salivate in private. I wiped my mouth on my sleeve and directed my attention to the wood-grain pattern of the laminate conference table. My mom patted my arm. The price of being a teen idol, right?

My mother had to sign the contract for me since I was still just fifteen, furthering my extreme embarrassment.

"Are you sure about this, honey?" she asked, cooing at me like I was a stupid baby.

My face got hot, and I felt like a child.

"Yeah, mom, I'm thure."

Great, one more thing to be embarrassed about: embodying my own pet peeve. I made the 'm' sound in 'mom' without closing my lips. Ugh. You know, like my big protruding buck teeth were in the way. I have the same hang-up about the 'b' and 'p' sounds — I hate it when people say words like 'baby' and 'purple' without touching their lips together. I think Gary Busey does that. I couldn't bear to watch him say something like 'my baby's purple bagpipes.' Makes my skin crawl. Anyway, yeah, it's weird, but, God, I hate that. And I hated the fucking transparent trays that covered my not-that-crooked teeth that made me do that. My teeth were fine. And the way my mom was calling me out in front of everyone, making them all look at me, not even trying to hide their smug grins — I wished I could just disappear.

This recoupable debt business, getting back to that wonderful topic, is unbelievable, in case you've never heard of it. It's something that no one likes to talk about. You think being a rock star means you have loads of cash, flash cars, and huge mansions, right? Well, ha! Sasha explained it to me and my mom right then and there.

"What happens," he said, "is like this: record company

gives band a million dollars in the form of advance. Out of advance, band pays for actually making album, which costs about half a million, when you figure studio time, engineers, plus housing for everybody and all that."

He scribbled those numbers in a column on his yellow legal pad.

"Then, there's manager, agent, and lawyer to pay, which add up to another hundred and fifty thousand out of that million."

He wrote some more numbers, performed a computation.

"See, that leaves, what, three hundred and fifty thousand to split? In our case, seven of us. I am in contract as a band member as well as manager. Oh, and, of course, I forgot to take out taxes."

He smacked himself in the head then and wrote on the pad. The other guys looked like they'd like to take a swipe at him as well, listening once again to this bullshit.

"Drop another hundred and seventy thousand. What are we down to? One-eighty? Split between seven people would be around twenty-five and change a piece. For whole year."

He spun the legal pad to our side of the table. It was ugly. My mouth dropped open, and I drooled down my chin.

He didn't need to state the obvious: that we all lived in L.A. and wanted to live the rock star lifestyle. Unbelievable. And the guys didn't want to give me an equal share, of course, because they hated my guts. Sharing with Damien, it looked like I was stuck working for minimum wage or even less. I was an indentured servant. I didn't feel too stellar.

'What about the royalties?' you say — 'cause that's what I said. Another ha! Joke's on you — I mean, *me*, rather. Remember that million dollar advance? That has to be paid back to the record company, which is why it's called an advance. Duh. Guess where the money to pay it back comes from. *Ding, ding, ding, ding!* You guessed it, sales. There's never much left over in the form of royalties. At least that's the way it was in In Dreams' early days, B.J. — before Jake.

Anyway, I don't want to bore you, but this being a rock star thing is kind of a scam when you're on the inside and not yet huge. Did you know that the band gets billed for everything? The food at the publicity photo shoots, the clothes, all those little four-dollar bottles of San Pellegrino that Damien loves. Then, there are lunches with the independent radio promoters... Oh! And don't get me started on those radio guys. Did you know that you have to *pay* to get your record played on the radio??? Go look up 'payola.' They say it doesn't exist anymore. Heaped up bullshit on a platter, I say.

On top of all that, there were band rules that I was instructed to strictly adhere to. Music, dance, and vocal lessons were just the beginning. I was supposed to work out at the gym with the band's personal trainer, maintain an 'enviable' suntan, submit to professional grooming each morning, eat only what was provided to me by the band's nutritionist, not be photographed going into or coming out of any clubs; there was to be no smoking, no drugs, minimal (if any) drinking (none in public), and no girlfriends (or boyfriends). We had a ten o'clock curfew, and I was to remain at the Chateau, sharing a suite with Damien, until space opened up and my belongings could be transferred to the Laurel Canyon house where the other guys lived.

Damien owned my ass. It was the perfect situation for him to ensure my silence on the Mary issue. At the end of that first business meeting, I realized the horrible truth of the situation: I was under band arrest.

Son. Of. A. Bitch.

I marveled at Damien's clever scheme.

All of my freedom had been taken from me. I couldn't even go back to school in the fall. Or smoke a bong. Or go up on the roof to draw. Or anything. Ever. I suddenly felt claustrophobic.

In the beginning, anyway. I never said a word about the night they kicked my ass. I just went on like it was business as usual, letting them reluctantly teach me shit. I was actually about to win over the other guys. Not that I wanted to. But it was essential. I think they respected the fact that I never whined about that beat-down even though I was in severe pain for weeks afterward.

The night after that first business meeting, when I was an official member of In Dreams, Damien and I drove up the hill again to celebrate with the other guys. Déjà vu touched me with an icy fist as we wound up the canyon. But things went much better this time. I got everyone stoned with the little stash of weed that I had left, and it instantly made me their best friend. They told me stories about stealing a mirror from Rosie O'Grady's Pub in Moscow, then hot-footing it away from cops with machine guns. I told them about watching Damien with his forbidden floozies. They laughed, flung their arms around me, and said I was OK. Assholes.

At least I finally got some of the dance moves down, thanks to those stoned fuckers. We would go out on tour, once I got up to speed on the songs. I had two months to learn everything. The best part? Girls were starting to notice me on the street, thanks to a blitzkrieg of PR. I was signing autographs by my second week. Trip out, man.

JAKE

Thursday, August 16 —

Friday, August 17

My days, jam-packed with weight lifting, hip hop dancing, and recording sessions, seemed to fly by, almost painlessly. But, the nights... Um, the nights were pretty bad. When the day was done, and I found myself in my alone in my room, a nightly nausea seized my core and would not let up. Eating dinner became insanely difficult. I lost weight, which was bad because I already looked anorexic to begin with. I had dark circles under my eyes from not sleeping. Every time I used the bathroom in my hotel room, I had to check behind the shower curtain to make sure there wasn't a body in the tub. I'd rip the beige curtain back with one shaking hand while shielding my eyes with the other. Whenever my new phone rang I jumped out of my skin. I took calls only from my mom and Sasha. My hands shook so bad that I had to give up drawing for a while, which was a real bummer, since sketching had always been my, I don't know, 'creative outlet,' I guess. I was not in good shape at all. The only thing that kept me going was playing the guitar. Damien gave me his black Strat, and I played it every night in my bed, minus the amp, sealing out the guilt and fright with distortions from the whammy bar.

One particular night during that time sticks in my mind as the absolute scariest night of my life. And that's saying a lot.

I climbed into bed and just could not sleep. I was high, as usual, but not that high. I had mostly come off the drugs for a number of reasons: 1) I was completely out of ecstasy, which had, of course, been my favorite; 2) I was so fucking tired from all the physical exercise they made me do every day; and 3) I got a better buzz from just walking around town with Damien and hearing chicks scream my name.

Anyway, this one night, after dinner with the guys at Kantor's, I set my guitar aside and lay in bed listening to the symphony of Sunset Strip: the intermittent hum of engines, punctuated by the occasional horn blast; the drunken buzz of industry drones blowing their meager wages on an evening at the overpriced bars lining the Sunset Strip; surprised obscenities and laughter wrung from the lips of nearly plowed-down pedestrians. It usually put me right to sleep, but not that night.

Over the muted din, I became aware of the fact that I could hear someone breathing. Right in my room. I looked around in the murky dark, trying to focus my eyes. A soft pink neon glow bled into the room from a six-inch gap between the heavy drape panels. I thought I must have been dreaming or something.

Someone unmistakably sighed. No doubt.

It sounded like it came from right next to me. A hissing sound, like air rushing out of a punctured tire, right in my ear. I jumped and peered around in the dim haze, my eyes as wide as they'd go, ignoring the stabbing pain that still screamed in my ribcage.

There. In the corner. Ohmygod. A sullen white face hovered next to the armoire. I sucked in a gasp and almost choked on my Invisalign mouthpiece. Elongated black holes materialized in the white circle where I'd expected to see eyes and a mouth. It was kind of like that Scream mask, but, I don't know, rounder and fuzzier, almost out of focus. No way.

Firmly convinced that I was seeing things, I crawled to the foot of my bed, my hand clamped over my aching ribs. As I got closer, the form sharpened into more of a face. Short blonde frizzy hair swam out of the dark like a faraway galaxy. I froze at the end of the bed, wanting to see, but not wanting to see. I stared and stared, waiting for it to move or speak or something. My heart raced. I could hear my new overpriced watch ticking.

It'snotrealit'snotrealit'snotreal. After some outrageously long time, the figure seemed to disintegrate right before my eyes, its particles sucked sideways into the wall. It was like watching a sand castle blow away from the top down. My ears settled upon the familiar noise of the street again, blotting out my ticking watch. I shook my head and dangled my feet over the edge of the bed. I stared at the void where the figure had stood. There was nothing there but shadows.

"It wasn't anything, lame-ass," I told myself in the dark. "Just your fucking imagination." I fell asleep in a puddle of drool.

The figure must have been a dream.

When I woke up, sunlight streamed through the gap in the curtains, and I was most definitely alone. My pillow was wet. I sat up and yanked out my torturous orthodontic device. On my way to the bathroom, something on the floor caught my eye.

A white triangle pierced the threshold beneath my locked door. I approached it with caution, recalling the ghost in the corner. I knelt to pick it up, my bruised hip popping. It was an envelope. Snow white. Addressed to me.

Who the hell would shove an envelope under my door? Surely not Damien or Sasha. But they were the only two other people with access to this doorway. Aside from the hotel workers. Maybe the maid's daughter was a fan or something.

I turned the envelope over and ran my finger under the flap, ripping it open. A pink sheet of paper was folded inside. I pulled it out and started to read.

"Dear John," it began, in swirly-curly-girly handwriting. "I am so *not* a huge fan of yours. I was so pissed when you joined In Dreams. I really want to know why you're doing this to Damien. You want attention? Oh, you're going to get it..."

Great, hate mail. I still thought it must have come from one of the hotel staff, since Sasha always brought the guys their fan mail to the studio. I wondered how this one had gotten through. I was kind of creeped out. But, on the other hand, momentous occasion — it was my first fan letter. Well, kind of. I read on, mostly out of curiosity.

"...I told them that she was with Damien that night, but they didn't believe me. They thought I was just making up some stupid little girl fantasy story..."

My blood went stone cold.

"...Did you see me in your room last night? I visited Damien, too, but he wouldn't look at me. He just sat there, crying over his stupid crack pipe. You ruined his whole fucking life, you piece of shit."

Um, security? I didn't have a security guard. None of the guys did. But, looked like it might be a good time to shake things up a little bit.

Or, wait — maybe I shouldn't say anything, I thought. I didn't really want to risk mentioning Patrick to Damien. I was kind of digging the whole pop star thing, in spite of the dancing and teeth straightening. Shit. What to do, what to do...

The letter was signed 'Love, Kelly,' followed by a heart with a jagged line down the middle.

And that was only the first letter of the day.

JAKE

Friday, August 17

And, so, with a spring in my step and a brand new fear in my heart, I met Damien in our living room and headed off to the lobby to wait for our ride. Sasha had told us he'd be a little late. I didn't breathe a word of my nightmare or the letter. Crazy. I was convinced that, just as I was getting a handle on the whole boy band deal, I had lost my mind. Great. Totally typical me.

Damien kept his eyes hidden behind a pair of mirrored Gucci shades. I was guessing his eyes were blood red behind them. An image of him sitting on the floor of his room, smoking crack and trying to ignore a ghost, materialized in my head. I stifled a giggle. I made a mental note to slip some PCP into his morning coffee. Douchebag.

Sasha picked us up and we got to the studio around eight thirty, which is super early for Hollywood. People normally don't get to work until about ten or eleven in 'the industry.' But, we were the super-clean eager beavers on the block, so there was an image to maintain. Or whatever. I was desperate for a smoke, and as it wasn't allowed in the building, I hit the men's room as soon as I had greeted the other guys and our producer.

The bathroom door opened soundlessly on a glassy expanse of charcoal marble. I crossed to the vanity, my heels making a sharp clicking sound that echoed off the tiled walls. I leaned against the counter with my back to the mirror and lit up. For a second, I wished for my own crack pipe, but my mind stuffed that thought as soon as it showed up.

I turned around and flashed a grimace, checking the progress of my shifting teeth in the mirror. I didn't see any difference yet, but my mouth sure hurt like a bitch. I took one big painful drag and smashed out my cigarette in the sink. Something caught my eye in the mirror. Something in one of the stalls. Someone. The door was ajar and I peered into the mirror, afraid to turn around and push the door in. I swear I saw a girl in that stall. Short black hair, black nightie-thing. I shook my head and looked at my own face. No time for this bullshit. Showtime.

"Ready to go, kid?" the producer asked as I strolled into the control room.

He clapped me on the back so hard I coughed. The blow sent orange sparks showering through my field of vision. I wondered if wrapping an elastic bandage around my mid-section would help. Fuck, you'd think I'd be all healed up by now. Anyway, he was big, that producer guy, like four hundred pounds or something. But, he had mad skills. He worked with people like 'N Sync, Justin Timberlake, the Backstreet Boys, Britney Spears before she wigged out, then Justin Bieber... That was why he cost so damn much.

"Yeah," I said, "let's hit it."

I opened the door and stepped into the sound booth. It smelled like pot, which, of course, made me crave some. I pulled on the old 1970s headphones and gave the guys on the other side of the glass the thumbs-up. I sang the first verse of the first song I was given lead vocals on and it sounded like shit. The guys looked at each other like something stank and the producer called for a short break. As I stepped out of the booth, Sasha's personal assistant came into the control room with a big canvas sack full of mail.

"Mail call," Sasha called out in a falsetto.

He passed out a couple of letters to Alex, a few to Scotty, more to Billy, a whole heap to Damien...

And one to me.

It was the first letter I'd gotten at the studio.

"Ha," Scotty laughed, pointing a drumstick at me, "little

dude scored his first fan letter."

They all laughed and razzed me about busting my fan letter cherry and all that. It was mildly embarrassing. What they didn't know was that I was scared to open the envelope. I tried my best to hide the fear.

White envelope, the security kind, with the blue criss-crossing lines on the inside. No return address, just a weird smiley face in the upper left-hand corner. My name on the front, written in a shaky scrawl, c/o my agent's name and address below that.

I saw a ghost in that wobbly print. My mind suddenly flashed on stories I'd heard on the news about letters containing anthrax. I shook my head, like that would help. My ears buzzed, my stomach churned, my palms sweated. I excused myself amid questions of "Are you alright, man?" So much for my new attempt at not showing fear.

I lurched down the hall to the men's room and slammed into a stall (there were no girls in the whole place that time; I checked). I stood there for a second, sick and dizzy with anxiety and dread. I ripped open the envelope and extracted a folded page, pinched gingerly between my thumb and forefinger.

No white powder — that was a good sign. At least I wasn't the target of a terror attack. That was a relief. I kind of chuckled to myself, thinking I was pretty funny sometimes. But, oh, Christ, my eyes fell on the unstable scrawl and suddenly, I didn't feel all that comical.

"I'm coming for you," it whispered.

PATRICK

August

Glaring white reflections, thousands of them, played upon the black surface of the Pacific and cut my eyes. I really fucking hate sunsets. Sunrises, too, for that matter. Up and down, up and down, on and off, day in and day out. Quit dicking around and make up your fucking mind already. You've only been at it forever. Idiot sun. Dark or light, it doesn't matter to me, but there should be a constant. Everything is more beautiful when it ceases to move.

Under the boardwalk, nobody bothers me. I watch the tide drift in and out as billions of grains of sand shift in an endless quest for a comfort or order that remains unknown to humans. People play and sunbathe yards from my hiding spot. Birds wheel around in random circles high above the whole scene. I get motion sickness just watching it all. I would stop it all if I could. Freeze everything, give all things and creatures the relief of arriving at a final destination.

I'm counting the minutes, waiting for that gutless little shit to set up my exhibit. I walk down Third Street, among the tourists in Santa Monica, every afternoon. I buy a paper, scan the art and entertainment section, absorbing the endless gossip about that fucking insipid boy band, as I eat my lunch on the Promenade, unnoticed, ignored.

No one looks at me. I look like hell. I haven't shaved in days. I haven't slept in even longer. My eyes are frightening, beginning to sink deeper into my skull. I wouldn't want to meet me in a dark alley. I don't wonder why no one looks at me. I'm scary as shit.

My face has been on the news, but they show an old publicity shot. I'm clean-shaven and smiling, apparently care-free. I was so uninspired then. Total dork. The cops are looking for me — that clean, smiling me — all over the city, probably all over the country. Finally, a little recognition.

But it's really nothing compared to how famous I will be in a few days. Provided that little shit, John, keeps his word. Jake, I mean. Pussy. I'll kill him if he screws me. Unless that weird little girl I met outside the record company beats me to it.

I want the fame, but hiding, right out in the open, feels good.

For now.

My star will shine.

JAKE

Late August

I saw some pictures in the paper of the artwork that was left behind in Patrick's apartment. It was good. I'm no art critic, but I know what I like. When I see a piece that really speaks to me, I kind of feel, I don't know, scared. It's almost like I can't stand to look directly at it, but I'm really drawn to it.

One time, when I was about eight or nine, my mom and my aunt took me to MOCA. I remember this big box set up in a gallery, all by itself, painted white on the outside, with little plywood steps leading up to a narrow doorway covered by a black curtain. The box might have been about seven, maybe eight feet high, and just big enough for one person to step into. I remember feeling a little anxious as I climbed up the steps. My mom and her sister had already taken their turns and were smiling encouragement as I looked over my shoulder at them.

What if there's something horrible inside, I wondered. What could be in there? The little title card said something about 'infinity.' I had a vague notion of that concept but couldn't imagine what a picture of it would look like. I imagined paintings of sideways number eights lining the walls of the box. Neither my mom nor my aunt had said there was anything scary inside. They came out okay after each spending a minute or so inside alone. I bent down and put on the gauzy shoe covers that slept in a box on the top step. I held my breath and slipped through the heavy black curtain into the unknown.

Little white Christmas lights twinkled all around me

behind a layer of smooth glass, each reflected a thousand times over in carefully angled mirrors and manufactured darkness. Man-made stars eternally suspended in a finite black void. I had a claustrophobic sense of free-falling in that tight space. There was no oxygen problem, but I felt winded and light-headed just the same. My heart beat fast, and I threw my hands over my eyes, squinting at infinity through a mask of intertwined fingers.

As primitive as that seems to me now, that was the first piece of art that really hooked me, gave me that kind of scared rush and got me interested in seeing more. That Infinity Box inspired a craving somewhere in my brain or soul... somewhere in me.

The same thrill hit me a couple of years later. On a field trip to the Getty, I saw a painting of a running dog by Francis Bacon, and I almost lost my mind. Like the Infinity Box, the painting occupied its own small gallery. As I entered the stark white room, the framed canvas seemed impossibly gigantic. And it was so dark. I thought of an oversized burn, seared into the wall by a giant's rectangular cigarette. I was afraid to look directly at it.

As I inched closer, I saw huge sweeping brushstrokes in a boundless black field, out of which the gray-white ghost of a dog could be seen running off to the right side. The entire image smeared upwards, as if it were being sucked up in parallel vertical lines by some unseen cosmic vacuum, equipped with some kind of rake attachment. I turned my head toward a blank white wall and stepped around the low-slung leather bench that was situated in the center of the echoing gallery space. I watched the ghost dog out of the corner of my eye, a leftover image from a vivid nightmare. Was it really there? Did someone really think that shit up? It totally tripped me out. I fell in love with art right then and there. Such power in one still image, first dreamed up, and then carefully shaped in two dimensions — a means of showing other people what was inside your head. Wild.

Concerts had a similar effect on the young me. The first concert I saw was the Cure at the Greek Theater. I was five. My mom took me, maxing out her credit card on the tickets. My reaction to the show made it worth it to her, she once told me. I begged her to buy me a keyboard or a guitar for weeks. She finally borrowed this old Yamaha keyboard from someone she worked with and brought it home for me to learn on. I taught myself a couple of Cure songs, and it was like medicine for my little soul, you know? I was kind of a sad kid, looking for a way to express myself, I guess. And music and art made me feel, I don't know, free or something. High. Happy?

I'd later get all those same sensations from drugs and spying on my neighbors. Looking back on everything, I'd say my head always felt like I'd smoked too much weed when I saw art or heard music that moved me. I loved that little rush of adrenaline or whatever chemical it was. It was exhilarating. I felt like I knew some kind of dark secret. And a piece of artwork or music does not have to be dark or scary in order to appeal to me; I get the same rush whether the piece features an electric chair or a beautiful sunset, a punk rock anthem or a symphony. Shock and awe.

Looking at Patrick's objects in the paper, I got a compelling nightmare feeling. Only it was mingled with an unfamiliar dread and shame. I felt sick and jittery, dead and alive.

A grainy shot of Mary's ulna with a Timex Ironman watch strapped to one end caught my attention first and took my breath away. Another picture showed a row of tongue cross-sections, four plates held in line by the disembodied latex-gloved hands of some L.A.P.D. forensic lab workers. I shuddered as my mind flashed on the memory of Patrick kneeling next to Mary with a pair of kitchen scissors, singing an old Roy Orbison tune as he cut. I remembered the first snip he made, severing that big thread that held her tongue down in the bowl of her lower jaw.

The sound it made was like a wire cutter through a slack guitar string.

The works shown in the paper were extremely ghoulish, and yet, I craved more. What had Patrick done after I took off? Did he complete enough work for a show? The article hinted that he had made more than enough pieces, but that there would be no show, of course.

I still had the key.

The one for Patrick's storage space.

DAMIEN

Sometime in August, Maybe September

What the fuck, man? I wish I knew what was going on with me, with my body, my head. I'm scared that I might be sick. Like, really sick. Might be the flu, like John said, but... I don't know.

Lately, I've been feeling like... I don't know, like I want to drink or get high all the time, you know? It is so weird. I never used to be this way. Drinking and drugs were never really allowed, unless, you know, we hung out at the house, but then it was just, like, a case of beer or two. Once in a while, I'd smoke with John out on my steps.

I don't know if this shit is physical or psychological. Might be depression. I haven't been to see my shrink since, you know, that night, The Incident. I'd better not go back to that guy, though. That dude thought I had issues before; I'd hate to hear what he thinks about me killing someone and then trying to keep it a big secret. I'm sure he'd tell me that I'm losing my mind and that I'd feel much better if I went to the cops. I don't think he could go to the cops himself, legally, I mean. There's that doctor-patient confidentiality thing, right? I could always leave John with Sasha, I guess, if I really want to talk to him. I'll have to think about it. I don't really have anyone else to talk to. Sasha already told me to shut up about it, so I can't talk to him. Lately, when I'm feeling good, I can kind of forget about it, which is great. Then I don't need to talk. Maybe getting high is a good thing. It's kind of like taking a little mental vacation.

But, then, sometimes, I like to go back and relive it.

John's stash is running low, he says. I don't want to believe that, but I know it's got to be true. We haven't been around the old neighborhood in a few weeks, so he hasn't seen his supplier or whatever you want to call him. Having to actually find stuff myself kind of freaks me out. I feel like some kind of degenerate or something.

I made John go with me over to Silver Lake last night. I know this girl who lives over there, and she always has some coke on her. She's kind of a low-life, but I'm getting to where I kind of need something once in a while.

"Hey," I said, standing on her crooked porch.

I leaned in to kiss her lips, but she turned away and all I got was cheek.

"Hi, Damien." She smiled and stepped back so John and I could enter the crumbling shack.

A patchy gray cat hissed at us from a dark corner as we stepped into the place.

Old vinyl records and cat toys littered the floor of the dimly lit living room. The low ceiling made me claustrophobic. An ancient air-conditioner hung in a side window, wheezing and spitting. The ammonia reek of cat piss permeated my every fiber.

"You must be Jake," she said, grinning at the kid. "You're cute."

That was really starting to annoy me — chicks digging John. Not that I was jealous, but... I was. I was the big star, not that skinny little dirtbag. I cracked my knuckles and put my arm around the girl.

"Hey, how about a kiss for your idol," I said to her.

She giggled and offered me her cheek again.

"So, Jake," she gushed, "you're new, huh?"

Typical new-age airhead, she had a knack for stating the obvious. She went to a dangerously tilting overloaded bookcase and took a mother-of-pearl box from the top shelf.

"You like to party, Jake?"

She opened the box, revealing a small bag of white

powder, a not-shiny razor blade, and cloudy glass straw.

"Yeah, well, I used to," John said, looking at the collection of records. "Hey, you mind if I play this?" he asked, holding up an Ozzy Osbourne LP.

The girl said he could play anything he wanted as she cut four fat lines on a ceramic coaster. She motioned for me to join her on the sofa, then put the straw to her nose. She sucked up two of the lines, threw her head back and laughed, holding the straw out to me. My turn.

I bent over the coaster, careful not to exhale so I wouldn't blow a single particle of the precious white powder away. I turned my head and then expelled all the air from my lungs. The tip of the straw touched the rim of my right nostril. I pinched off the left one with my left index finger. I guided the other end of the straw to the edge of the coke line. With a mighty burst of suction, I inhaled the much-too-short ridge. I repeated the procedure using my left nostril. The straw dropped from my hand, and I sat back on the couch, grinning. I grabbed the coaster, licked a finger, and brushed the remaining dregs into a little pile, which I scrubbed on my teeth. The hot tingle began directly between my newly waxed eyebrows and washed through my body from the top down as Ozzy screeched about going off the rails.

The girl's friend showed up shortly after that, and we headed out to Space Land. Parking's a bitch over there, but it's dark with good music and minimal press — I like it. I knew John and I weren't supposed to be out at a club, especially at this hour, but, fuck it — I'm a rock star. We said our hellos to some industry types (no one I recognized, thank God) and huddled in a shadowy corner.

The girl's friend wore an old school coke spoon on a chain around her neck. Looking at it, I couldn't stop licking my lips. Seriously, I think I got chapped lips within the space of five minutes or something. Anyway, the friend pulled out a little glass vial of white powder. Man, it was my lucky night. I snatched it out of her hand and ran for the bathroom, leaving John unattended. Dumb, on my part, I know — I was kind of starting to trust him, but certainly not enough to leave him alone in a public place. But, I really needed the hit, you know? The last one was wearing off fast.

So, I went into the bathroom and pulled a guy out of a stall. Since he was on his way out anyway, I didn't see the big deal, but he recognized me and said he was going to kick my ass. I told him to fuck off and slammed the metal door *sans* lock. Layer upon layer of graffiti told me that Fugazi Rocks and Pete is a Fag! and other meaningless bullshit. There was nothing written about me; people who hung at Space Land didn't even know boy bands existed (except for that one dude who wanted to kick my ass, I guess). My feelings were just a little bit hurt, but I'd get over it.

I emptied out the vial on top of the metal toilet paper holder box and snorted like a preschooler with a nose full of snot.

Cold. I coughed. I leaned against the cool metal door and waited for the rush. I didn't feel anything for a few minutes. I heard the band tuning up on stage.

My tongue went numb. My cheeks got all hot and tingly. I took a couple of deep breaths and felt light-headed and silly. Magic. I wished for another vial.

When I got back to the table, miracle of miracles, John was still there. Fool. If I were him, I would've been so out of there. He's okay, that kid. When he's not stealing my spotlight.

"Hey, sorry, kid," I said to him, "but I didn't save you any."

I kissed one of the girls. Then I kissed the other one. John handed me a drink, a gin and tonic.

"No problem, man," he said. "I didn't want any anyway. Here, have a drink. I kind of like this 'no-such-thing-as-underage-when-you're-a-star' thing."

He grinned like a dope.

We listened to the band for a while, then headed out for

some piano bar music at the Dresden. I like the really old school places, you know? So fucking cheesy but totally fun. After we got there, the girl with the coke gave me another bump, John bought me a bunch of drinks, and I don't remember much after that. I guess John got me into the car, and the driver brought us back to the hotel.

That's where I woke up, anyway, the hotel.

JAKE

Saturday, September 1

Damien pulled his silver Boxster into a parking space behind Santa Monica Storage. The postage stamp lot was empty except for two other cars.

"I'll be right back," I said, climbing out without opening my door. He thought I was getting some folding chairs for my mom.

"Take your time, but, you know, hurry up," Damien said, brushing my footprint off the passenger seat.

He was hung over and jonesing for some smack, whether he realized it or not.

"You sure you don't need a hand?"

"No, I'm good."

I forced a slow swagger across the blacktop and slid the key into the building's side door. I stepped inside and looked for the locker number on the directional sign that hung from a couple of chains above my head. I took off down a corridor to the right, looking over my shoulder.

I stood in front of the locked storage unit, sweating some pretty major pit stains in my Armani Exchange hoodie. I swallowed hard and hoped I wouldn't pass out in there with the door wide open. Footsteps echoed in the corridor perpendicular to the hall I was in. The sound crashed off of the orange and white painted cinder block walls and battered my nerves. A young woman in high heels appeared in the junction, pushing a stroller. She jumped when she saw me. That made us even. I jumped higher, actually. She had short black hair — yeah, I thought she was Mary.

"Hi," she managed.

I lifted a hand and smiled in response. She looked at me like she wanted to say something more, but instead she just marched on. I exhaled in relief. I was in no mood for conversation.

I flashed on my grandfather's funeral for a second. The storage place reminded me of one of those cemetery mausoleums where the caskets are all stacked up in drawers along the walls of a highly polished marble maze. In this storage place, you didn't know what was stacked up behind the walls. Dull cement and bright orange steel beams took the place of glossy stone and floral wreaths. A chill raised the hairs on the back of my neck.

I poked my key into the lock and pushed the door open. The darkness sharpened my senses, highlighting my anxiety. I stepped inside and groped for a light switch on the wall. A bare bulb threw a harsh glare on mountains of blue plastic painter's tarps. I stood there for a while, feeling my heart beat in my throat, listening for footsteps to rescue me from facing the horror that I knew lay beneath the covers.

No one came to save me.

A pale hand reached out in front of me, trembling ever so slightly, and grabbed at the closest tarp. The hand was mine, but I had somehow detached it from my conscious self. I pretended not to feel the slick plastic whooshing beneath my cold sweaty fingers. I made believe that I really was looking for folding chairs. Nope, no chairs here. Just some fish tanks and junk.

I drew a harsh breath and tugged the cover off of one heap and found myself eye-to-eye with one of Mary's baby blues. I jumped, but I did not scream. It took a few seconds for my mind to process what I was seeing. A long arrow pierced one round naked eyeball and held it fixed within a liquid-filled vitrine. The tip of the arrow stuck in a target, just to the left of the bull's eye. The optic nerve floated upwards from the back of the eyeball, as if reaching for air.

Housed in a glass box below that, some unidentifiable piece of meat was sculpted into what might be... a bunny? What the hell was that? I leaned closer to the glass, my nose almost touching it. It wasn't a bunny. It wasn't any kind of sculpture. Up close, I could see that it was a complete muscle, the fibers on one end frayed and separated, kind of like some freaky sea anemone. I wrestled the tarp back onto the pile of revulsion and sagged against the wall, tasting bile and wishing for my bed.

He had totally disassembled her, exploded her parts like he was making some kind of psycho killer technical manual. I'm not sure why, but I was shocked at the mental image. I had seen him doing it, had seen pictures in the paper, but, here it was, again, right in front of me. It was real.

Footsteps echoed in the other hallway.

Closer.

My heart pounded.

Closer still.

Shock and panic dried my throat and moistened my eyes. I thought about slamming the door shut, but I was too slow.

The footsteps came to a dead stop at the doorway. I heard something shift behind me. Breathing.

Every hair on my body stood at attention.

"You little cocksucker."

My blood turned stone cold.

Water dripped somewhere down the hall.

My scalp tingled. Fight or flight.

There was no way out of the storage unit.

"Patrick," I whispered, turning to face him, willing my mouth into a lopsided grin. "Wow. Man, it's good to see you."

His bangs covered one eye, as usual, but the other had a hard glint to it, surgical stainless steel. "You scared the piss out of me."

I coughed out a nervous laugh. It fell flat.

"Listen, this is some fantastic shit, man."

I waved a hand in the general direction of the tarps.

He didn't say anything.

"They... they grabbed me...," I stammered.

His eye narrowed. He looked rough. A couple days' stubble clung to his cheeks, bags hung from his eyes, and he smelled bad, like b.o. and mothballs.

"Set up my show, you little fucker. I know where you went. Boy band pop star. You can use new big name to draw them in. You tell them who made the stuff, tell them who the artist really is or..."

He stopped to listen. It was then that I noticed the straight razor in his hand. It was folded, but I recognized the ivory handle from his bathroom counter. Panic hit me in the chest.

More footsteps clattered in the hallway.

Patrick's eyes never left mine, but I was sure he saw my hand move as I fingered my cell. I couldn't stop myself from moving, though I knew that it would probably be in my best interest to do so. Involuntarily, I looked down at my phone. He held his silence as I discovered that I had no bars in this little dungeon. I cursed under my breath.

The footsteps came to a halt at the door, directly behind him. The woman with the stroller stood in the corridor, her little kid smiling at me, clapping her chubby hands. Patrick slid the razor into his pocket.

"Hey, I'm really sorry to interrupt," the woman said to me with a sheepish smile. "I was wondering... Aren't you the new In Dreams guy, Jake?"

She glanced at Patrick, wrinkling her nose a little at the sight of him, then, went right on gushing at me.

"Gosh, you know, being from here, I never ask anyone, but could I please, please have your autograph?"

I heaved one heavy-assed sigh and smiled. I would have fallen down and melted in total relief, if I hadn't been leaning against a wall. I stepped around Patrick and took the lady's hand.

"Yes, I am Jake. I'd be happy to sign an autograph."

Shit, that was, without a doubt, the absolute happiest moment of my life.

"You got a pen? My friend and I were just leaving, anyway."

She rummaged around in her giant purse as Patrick gave me one last seething glare.

"Okay, John," Patrick said, emphasizing my real name, which, for some reason, raised my hackles. Guess I didn't like being reminded of the loser I used to be. Huh, I hadn't noticed until that moment.

"You set that up and give me a call, okay?"

He laid a hand on my shoulder.

I recoiled.

"Sure, you got it, man," I said, pulling free from his cold claw and accepting a Sharpie and an address book from the woman. "Ma'am, why don't I sign this for you outside?"

Patrick took off down the corridor, while I locked up and sailed away with the woman and her little girl back towards Damien and the car, a genuine smile playing on my lips."I am so sorry to bug you," she said, "but I am the biggest In Dreams fan, and you are the best thing that has ever happened to them."

"Hey, no worries. I totally appreciate that. I'm glad you came along. I didn't really want to talk to that guy anyway," I said. "Now, what's your name, darling?"

JAKE

Last Week of September

With our first show coming up in just over a month, things were falling into place very nicely. Damien stumbled and drooled everywhere, barely holding his shit together. In typical showbiz style, everyone around us, as long as they were getting paid, pretended not to notice.

Our limo pulled up at the KROQ building at seven thirty-four a.m. Damien threw the door open, gave a long deep retch, and spewed steaming yellow bile into the gutter. Luckily, there were no photographers skulking around, for a change. The dude was totally hurting. I wanted to laugh my ass off, but I bit my tongue and did my best to maintain a caring and concerned appearance. For the time being. I was a good actor after all.

"Damien," Billy bitched, stepping over the vomit and onto the curb with an exaggerated reach of his foot, "you really need to get a grip, darling. You're quickly becoming our very own Courtney Love."

"True dat," Alex agreed, jumping out and touching his fist to Billy's on the sidewalk.

I walked behind Damien and guided him toward the glass door.

"You'll be alright, man," I whispered to him. "You just need a little pick-me-up, that's all."

Once inside the building, I steered him to the men's room and slapped some cold water on his face. He slumped against me and slid off my leather jacket like an egg off a Teflon pan. His knees thunked on the black tile, and his teeth clicked together. He crawled into an open stall, smacking his head on the toilet, grabbing blindly for a hand-hold. After he vomited once more and dry-heaved a bunch, I pulled out my trusty old pipe and the all-healing white rock. Damien inhaled like he was trying to suck a golf ball through a garden hose. He slumped in the corner, forearm over his eyes. Seven seconds later, his eyes flew wide, and he let out a piercing whoop, pumping his fist in the air.

"Whooooooo! Let's rock and roll, boy," he yelled, arching his eyebrows.

I swaggered along behind him as he burst into the studio, reborn, at least for the moment.

His portion of the interview was totally abysmal, as usual. Those days, DJs and reporters would interview Damien, and he'd completely lose track of what he was talking about or even where he was. He'd ramble on and on about the most random shit, like ghosts and groupies. A couple of times, I was absolutely positive that he was about to confess what he did to Mary. I was more than a little unnerved on those occasions (read: I was shitting Sacagawea dollars), but for the most part, I thought it was pretty fucking hilarious. Priceless. Rumors of an imminent return to rehab made the rounds, of course, as embarrassing pictures of him completely wrecked outside clubs began to appear.

I could not have been happier.

What did I do, you ask? I played the part of concerned best friend and stayed the hell out of the pictures. I gave him drugs whenever he asked and sometimes when he didn't. I wasn't using much so that I could dedicate my dwindling stash to keeping him loaded. I told him that chicks still dug him, that he looked fabulous, and that he was the force that drove the band. I told him whatever he wanted to hear. It did far more damage, and was a lot more fun, than telling him the sad truth, which was In Dreams didn't need his sorry ass. It was all a big game to me.

Sasha, in the meantime, had become my new best friend. He liked the way I had learned, with lightning speed, to sweet-talk the media, my new ability to make the lamest dance moves look cool, my genuine musical ability, and the way I made girls swoon. In his mind, it was a definite plus that girls frequently mistook me for Brandon Flowers or Chris Carraba — he was always there to handle the overflow of groupies. He and I got along just fine. I knew his vision was obscured by the dollar signs that had practically replaced his pupils, but I liked having him on my side anyway.

Noticing Sasha's increasing goodwill towards me, the other guys began to see me as something more than the weed guy. They let me hang with them when they went to the beach or out shopping and included me in their inside jokes (most of them slamming Damien by then). They encouraged me to write songs, too, which was really cool. I felt like I was being recognized for a real talent, you know? I felt, I don't know the right word, validated? Fulfilled? Good. Mostly.

To be totally honest, I did start to feel lonely and restricted, too. I came to resent the endless rules I was forced to live by. I spent a lot of time in my bed, fantasizing about ways to break out of the Prison of Pop I'd found myself in. As babyish as it sounds, I missed my mom. I loved my new life and the possibilities that it brought, but I missed my old life, too. I know, weird. But, whatever, it was real, and I had to deal.

Damien was in no shape to keep up his role as my guardian, so I began to push the limits of the band rules as far as I possibly could. I smoked but not in public. I took the guys to clubs but came home in time for curfew. I ate fast food. I started to get the hang of living large, even if it was recoupable. I had custom suits made, I ordered food to be delivered from some of the most expensive restaurants, sent random girls jewelry. And I charged it all to the band's credit cards. What's the worst they could do, kill me? Ha. Not bloody likely.

With my newly cropped hair, cobalt blue contacts and killer smile, I brought the band more girls than they'd ever had. With my talent, I brought them authentic musical skills and credibility. Just being who I was, I brought them hope for a brighter future and ever increasing cash flows. I kept my haunted misery to myself.

They all looked at me with dollar signs in their eyes.

I wore mirrored shades.

JAKE

Sunday, September 30

Kings of Leon blasted from my cell, heralding a call from my mom.

"Hey, Mom, what's up?" I said into my Bluetooth thing-amajig.

I loved walking down the street with that thing. People would think I, the famous pop star, was talking to them. Then they'd notice the earpiece, and they'd go tomato red and slink away. Too funny. I was in my room now, though, so there was no one to look cool for.

"Hey, honey."

I could tell from the tremor in her voice that she had bad news. My first thought was my grandmother. My second thought was Patrick. My stomach turned sour.

"I just got a letter in the mail from the landlord."

Relief. I mean, I knew it wasn't good news, but I was relieved because it wasn't anything about Patrick.

"It's finally happening. The bastard finally wised up and is kicking us out so he can renovate."

"Crap," I breathed.

I may have been Mr. Just-on-the-verge-of-total-idol-atry, but I didn't have any cash. As I've said, the record company paid for everything — well, loaned money to the band for stuff, anyway. And I doubted they'd give me anything to help my mom, especially after my recent shopping sprees.

Mom said the rent controls no longer applied and that the landlord felt he was entitled to more cash. After all, he did own a prime swath of property in mega-trendy downtown. He gave my mom thirty days to get out. Not thirty days to come up with more money, but thirty days to actually vacate the premises. He was going to knock down the whole damn building. Big surprise.

My mom clearly needed a place to live. She had been staying at my grandmother's the past couple of weeks, but she had just sold Grandma's house. She needed the money to pay for the nursing home Grandma was moving into at the end of the month. The sale would close in less than thirty days. Great, I'd have to handle this. My parental duties apparently hadn't stopped just because I had hooked up with a world-famous band. I said good-bye and walked out into the suite's sitting room.

In one of his more lucid moments, I went to Damien. He said we'd get paid in December, and he was in the same situation as me. Fucking useless. As far as I was concerned, he became more obsolete by the minute. I asked him if I could get some kind of advance or something from someone so my mom would have a place to live. He put his crack pipe down just long enough to tell me that I'd have to talk to Sasha.

I knew Sasha saw potential in me, but I didn't know if he'd lend me money. Thinking and hoping someone can make you rich is one thing; lending that same unproven asshole cold hard cash is something entirely different.

When Sasha dropped in on me and Damien at our hotel that night after dance rehearsal, I saw my chance to plead my case. I felt kind of weird about it. I was never a beggar, you know. But, hey, I never asked to be in this fucking band in the first place. They fucking owed me.

I slouched in a chair opposite Sasha in our cluttered living room area. I tilted my head and studied his face as he diddled his BlackBerry. He finally felt my eyes on him and glanced over at me.

"Something on your mind, *da*?" he asked.

I eyed his clothes. I'd never seen him dressed so casually, to put it nicely. He was wearing jeans and a T-shirt with the sleeves ripped off. Very unusual and a little... well, icky. The vaporous white shirt hugged his bloated gut, and his doughy arms hung bare like unbaked bread.

He had recently gotten a new tattoo. His first. I'd heard him talk about it, but this was the first time I'd actually seen it. Yeah, he was almost fifty, but, what the hell, right? Personally, I thought the whole ink thing was played out — I had a tattoo myself, but I was fifteen, not fifty. But what did I know? Anyway, it was supposed to be a sun, but to me, it looked like a ripped and bleeding sphincter. I thought he would live to totally regret that thing. When he turned seventy, and the red faded to pink, all his shuffleboard-playing friends would badger him about the bloody asshole on his shoulder. Too funny.

He had a new girlfriend, too, which I believe had something to do with the new tattoo and the stab at what he thought were fashionable clothes. I'd seen the chick at a couple of our rehearsals. He thought she was smoking hot — ratted-out white hair, skinny, skanky — like a shagged-out stripper or something. She reminded me of a ripped and bleeding sphincter, too.

In any case, I was hoping Sasha's new casual attitude would mean he'd be receptive to a request for fundage. I swallowed hard, took a deep breath, and attempted a smile.

"Listen, Sasha," I said. "I could really use some, uh, cash, you know."

He looked up from his phone.

Nothing grabs your attention like somebody asking you for money.

I cleared my throat. "I know I've only been with you guys for a couple months, but, see, my mom..."

Apparently, I had way underestimated my value. Dude gave me plenty of cash to lease a place for my mom over in the Valley, plus get her some new furniture. Sweet. I mean, the place isn't a castle or anything, but it's nice and quiet and close to Grandma's old folks' home. And — giant plus — Patrick doesn't know where she is. Not that I thought he'd ever grab her or anything, but the thought had occurred to me. (Okay, I'd fantasized endlessly about him grabbing her and holding her for ransom or some shit, but I don't want to talk about that.)

My success with getting cash out of Sasha sparked a dangerous new confidence. I truly believed that I was suddenly worth millions. Hungry for more money, fame, and attention — and with Patrick on my mind, of course — I paid a visit to the old neighborhood. I told Damien I was going to see my mom. He was so ripped that he barely acknowledged me, but he did make Sasha drive me. Prick.

Leaving Sasha in the car with his BlackBerry, I went to see Mr. Fawlty, the owner of the gallery that Patrick had been scheduled to show at before the whole Mary fuck-up occurred. Sasha waited for me in the car. I walked through the empty gallery toward the back and found a thin, gray-haired man in a black turtleneck in a small office, looking at slides. I cleared my throat, and he turned to face me.

"Mr. Fawlty?" I asked.

He peered over his half-moon glasses and confirmed my accusation.

"Listen, I was wondering if you might be interested in helping me put on a show."

He looked me up and down, scrutinizing my every line, plane, and edge.

"What kind of show might that be, young man?"

He didn't recognize me.

"I'm a…" I stopped myself before the word *friend* could crawl out of my mouth. "…an acquaintance of Patrick Salinger's." My heart thumped as I spat out the name.

Fawlty removed his glasses and set them carefully on his immaculate desk along with the slide projector remote.

He looked carefully at my face. He knew who I was.

"I see."

That was all he said for at least a whole minute.

I didn't know if I should turn around and leave or what. He was kind of a weird guy. Reminded me of Vincent Price.

He finally continued. "Yes, I've been expecting you. I understand we could put on quite a show, thanks to our friend."

I didn't know anything about the art world, but I didn't care for the vibe this guy was giving off. I looked around his modern minimalistic office. It felt sterile, like an operating room. I tried to avoid meeting the guy's burning green eyes, but I could feel them searing into me. I cleared my throat and looked directly at him. I didn't know if he was waiting for me to say something, but the silence was getting pretty weird. It was a mistake, going there.

"So, um," I said. "What do we do?"

He stood behind his desk and shuffled a neat stack of papers, finally choosing one to read silently. Seconds ticked by. I stood there, waiting. I thought he must have been testing me or something. Weirdo.

"When do we do the show?" I finally ventured.

Fawlty lifted his eyes again to my forehead, wearing a bored expression.

"Mr. Thomas, I am aware that you are about to become one of the most famous young men in the world," he said as he picked a tuft of imaginary lint off of his black sweater and mimed dropping it into the steel mesh wastebasket. "This was something Mr. Salinger and I did not foresee when he made his agreement with me; therefore certain adjustments will need to be made to our contract."

He looked at me like I was supposed to say something. So, I did.

"Uh-huh."

He snort-laughed at me like that didn't quite meet his expectations. I felt my face getting hot.

"John," he said, rocking back on his heels, hands behind his back. "I want to use your name as artist, instead of Patrick's. What do you think of that?"

I thought that was fucking great! I always wanted to be an artist. Patrick wouldn't like it, but, so what? I didn't want to let on that I was too stoked, so I bit the inside of my cheek to keep from grinning.

"Yeah, okay."

"My dear boy, I have worked with many celebrities, and I do require a higher commission on their sales. Due to higher overhead, of course, accommodating larger crowds and what have you."

Um, I wasn't sure what 'overhead' was. But, he wanted more money — I got that. I didn't like where this was going. I wanted the money. Shit, I earned it.

"Forty percent, Mr. Thomas, and your opening shall coincide with your concert debut in order to capitalize on media interest."

"You mean I get to keep forty percent of the money?"

I was so dumb.

He raised an eyebrow.

"Yes, forty percent."

Scam.

"Um," I said, thinking dimly that I was getting screwed, "I'm not sure I like that idea."

I thought about it for a second. I'd get forty percent, and this shit could sell for millions! I changed my mind and thought that was a fantastic deal. But, I paused a little longer for dramatic effect. Heh.

"I could always have the show somewhere else," I said.

I thought I was an expert negotiator. Man, I was a retard. I was getting screwed.

Fawlty laughed. "Mr. Thomas, Patrick and I have an understanding that involves issues you may not be aware of." He pursed his lips. "I'd hate to be forced into getting the authorities involved in this simple matter."

He tipped his head back and raised an eyebrow.

"I am prepared to offer you sixty percent of sales, provided you say nothing about the show to anyone without the proper representation, and you claim the works as your own. I will pay all added security costs your presence will require, out of my own pocket."

Stupid me, this was what he had offered me in the first place. Duh.

Anyhow, I didn't like it. Patrick had promised that I'd get all the cash. But I thought this guy might go to the cops if I didn't take the deal. What did he have to lose? He gave me a contract and told me to return it to him at my earliest convenience.

I was dismissed.

JAKE

Wednesday, October 3

I snuck out of the hotel while Damien was passed out. We'd had another long night of partying over on Vermont. I walked right out the front door of the hotel and down the block to the local record store. It was my first real taste of real freedom since the night of The Mary Incident.

I walked into the shop and headed straight for the CD racks. I checked out how many copies of the In Dreams CD they had in stock. We didn't have our own section yet, so I had to look under the generic 'I' tab. Two copies. Hmmm.

There was a fat blond girl on the other side of the rack, pretending to gaze at something behind me. She looked kind of familiar, but I couldn't place her. I felt a little scared, but I wasn't sure why. Just a little paranoid, I guessed, being out on my own.

I turned my attention back to the paltry 'I' section. It was disappointing. I'm not sure what I expected, but two stinking CDs? Weak. I guess I had thought of Damien as a hot-shot pop star, you know, a couple of weeks ago, before all this shit happened. Things aren't always what they seem, I guess.

Walking toward the front of the store, I saw a poster on display, featuring my five band mates, all half-naked and shiny-looking. Ew. It reminded me that we were due to take a photo for a new poster tomorrow afternoon. I wondered if I would be slathered with oil or something. Guess I'd find out.

As I stood at the magazine rack, flipping through a

music mag, I felt someone standing next to me, like they were waiting for something. I looked up, thinking maybe I was in the person's way, blocking the guitar magazines or something. A group of three girls stood there, staring at me, huge anticipatory smiles plastered on their beautiful faces. One of them suddenly lunged at me, grabbing my arm.

"Oh, my God," she gushed. "Look who it is! Gina, take my picture!"

She handed her phone cam over to the one she called Gina. They oohed and aahed as I blew through embarrassment and proceeded directly to enjoyment.

"You look great — really, a lot younger than you do on TV," Gina told me.

Younger? I tilted my chin upward and gave her my best smoldering look. I hoped I didn't look as goofy and awkward as I felt.

The third girl, a pudgy little redhead, giggled and sidled up to me for her turn, holding a pen and a piece of paper out for me to sign. A few other shoppers looked over at us with cool curiosity. (FYI: approaching celebrities in Hollywood isn't really cool, unless you're a tourist from the Midwest or something. Hollywood is our home turf, so we expect people to be cool and give us our space.)

Anyway, as I signed, with a growing crowd watching, 'All my love, Jake xxx,' on Red's paper, she said: "Oh, my God, you know 'Mr. Brightside' is my most favorite song ever!"

Ouch.

JAKE

October

The photo shoot was awful, as I'd expected. Having make-up applied to my face was as hellish as I'd always thought it would be, but when the make-up artist made me take off my shirt so she could do my upper body... that was damn humiliating. I mean, it was bad enough that I was nowhere near as buff as the other guys, but I also still had shadows from that gigantic bruise on my rib cage. It had mostly cleared up, but you could still see the crimson out-line, even after all those weeks. She asked me what hap-pened and, with the other guys all leaning forward in their make-up chairs, staring at me, I told her that I'd gotten into a bar fight.

"Funny, I haven't read about you being in any fights. You shouldn't hang out in Silver Lake, though, hon," she said with a wink.

Busted. Shit, that meant that she'd seen me and Damien out on the town.

The rest of the day, I sweated through about thirteen different designer outfits and asked if I would be allowed to keep the leather jacket that I had posed in. I mean, the band paid for renting all that shit through 'recoupable ex-penses,' and since I wasn't seeing much cash, I figured I might as well get some clothes out of the deal. Not only did I keep the jacket, but I swiped a nice pair of Armani jeans as well. I would have nicked the shoes I wore to complete the outfit, but the other guys didn't like that idea. I was already pressing my luck.

◇ ◇ ◇

As Damien continued his downward spiral into the fun house called drug addiction, I sped along an opposite trajectory. I had developed an addiction to wheat grass and working out. Girls screamed and swooned wherever I went, Sasha talked to me about the importance of leading a hugely popular boy band and also of 'individual creative development' (aka, a solo career!), and, lastly, the other guys in the band totally trusted me. Instead of looking to Damien for ideas in the recording studio, they came to me.

In direct proportion to their advances, Damien retreated. He rarely talked to me, unless he was in need of drugs. My stash had finally run out, so I found myself on the streets of West Hollywood, hiding beneath my heavy winter coat and darkest shades at 2 a.m., buying stuff from other junkie musicians to feed Damien's growing habit. He had trapped me and basically kept me as a prisoner, so, you know, turnabout is fair play, right?

I was in control. I had gradually grown out of my fear of being hunted down by Patrick or picked up by the cops. It felt good, liberating. My new concerns were much more fun. The things that scared me most were girls ripping my clothes and photographers catching me sneaking beers up at the Universal City Walk. I found that I could party anywhere I wanted as long as I stayed away from the paparazzi. The most beautiful thing of all was my new realization that Patrick couldn't do anything to me. That was the best part about never being alone. Even when I was buying drugs, I had a driver who waited for me with the engine running. I was totally safe.

Our first performance was six days away. We'd be headlining at the freaking Staples Center, man, blocks from the old neighborhood. I couldn't fucking believe it. I had every word of every song down, and I absolutely rocked each and every dance routine. I was a Rock Star, baby.

The Staples Center performance would kick off the In Dreams 'Resurgence' tour, which would take us to thirty-nine cities in forty-six days. I was told that the pace would be fast and furious, and we'd be in super close quarters. The tour would serve as my introduction to living with Billy, Alex, Scotty, and Reggie. I'd move into the Laurel Canyon house with them after the tour. Heh. We'd see how long they'd be able to keep up their goody-two-shoes bullshit with me around. I was ready to fucking unleash the beast; quit wearing my retainer and everything.

On top of my music career taking off, I had a big art show coming up. Yeah, it was supposed to be Patrick's, but you know what? That show was mine now. Fuck him. I always wanted to be an artist — I was taking full advantage of the opportunity. Having an over-the-top exhibit opening the same night I debuted with In Dreams would make me the world's biggest superstar.

Hey, I earned it, so fuck you, too.

With Damien strung out and sleeping all day, I had Sasha drive me over to the storage place and then over to Fawlty's gallery, Gallery 551. He helped me carry a couple of pieces inside and stood beside me, gaping at the work.

"So, you did this work?" Fawlty asked in mock surprise when I showed him a cubic vitrine containing a cross sectioned brain.

He winked at me. It was part of the game. The story he'd devised was that I, inspired by my neighbor's grisly behavior, latched onto his ideas and carried his plan to fruition with artificial substances standing in for real body parts. And Fawlty, ever eager to take a chance on edgy, socially relevant art, gave me a chance as an expression of his sorrow over Mary. A small (miniscule) percentage of the proceeds from sales generated by the exhibition would go to a scholarship fund set up by the girl's parents. A large percentage would go to me, and an even larger percentage would go to Mr. Fawlty himself. I hadn't signed the contract, though. I was holding off on it as long as I possibly could. Maybe he'd forget that I hadn't given it to him, and I could somehow finagle a better deal later. What do you want? I was a stupid kid.

"Sure, it's mine," I said, watching him examine the piece from every angle. "I know Patrick told you that I had some of his stuff, but what happened was, see, he took off because he was afraid of the cops, and they took everything he made before he could have his show. I read the story in the paper and quick came up with this stuff as a sort of tribute to my sicko friend."

I could play along. I was practicing the story, trying to solidify it into a believable truth.

"Hmmm... This is very Damien Hirst, young man. I believe you'll do quite well. How many pieces are in your collection?"

Then, he put a hand up to his mouth and whispered: "The letter from our friend says he made seven items."

I filled him in on the seven pieces, still trying to get my story straight. I didn't want to be tripping over my words when I had to talk to the press. I would show seven of the twelve items I had in my possession. We would go ahead with the opening next Friday, as planned. The artist's reception would begin at five o'clock, so I could be in time for stage call at eight, right down the street at the Staples Center.

I thought Fawlty was going to ask for the contract then, but he didn't.

That whole Friday night would be a public relations coup. Sasha practically pissed his pants standing beside me at the gallery. He was already counting the money. It would be a debut like no other.

JAKE

Last Week of October

I got another letter.

Sasha hand delivered it to me at the recording studio. White security envelope, smiley face in the upper left-hand corner, my name in wobbly print. My ears buzzed, my stomach churned, my palms sweated. Déjà vu. I raced down to the men's room and ripped it open.

"Dear Igor, Fawlty told me," it whispered in Patrick's anesthetized voice.

Fuck. Fawlty *told* him? Told him what? Okay. I took a deep breath and considered the implications. Fawlty told Patrick about the exhibition. What could that mean? WTF, man?

I decided to take the direct route and confront Fawlty. I pulled out my phone, dialed 411, and was connected to the gallery.

"Gallery 551," Fawlty cooed.

"You told Patrick?" I breathed.

"Ah, John," Fawlty said. "How are you, good sir? Shall I call you Jake, now? Are you getting excited?"

"What do you want?" I asked.

"Money, of course, my dear boy. Isn't everything about money these days?"

He sounded nauseatingly cheerful. What did he know about me? I felt things beginning to spin out of my control.

"How much?" I asked.

"All of it," he answered. "Well, I'll give a little to that

scholarship fund, of course, per the agreement, but wouldn't you be much more comfortable letting me have the rest? After all," he purred, "you've come out of a very nasty situation quite well, wouldn't you say?"

I swallowed hard. My eyes rolled around the lavatory. I was willing to part with the money. I mean, I wanted it, and I kind of needed it, but my personal security had just jumped into the spotlight. Everything could come crashing down at any second if Fawlty knew too much and decided he didn't want to work with me. Fuck, I got scammed.

Patrick had originally told Fawlty to give me all the money, didn't he? Or was that just for some second show? I'd never actually seen the original letter that Patrick gave him, so I couldn't really count on anything.

I could just tell him to put Patrick's name on the show and back out.

Aw, fuck that noise.

I wanted to be an artist. All bets were off. I'd have to deal with Fawlty. I'd just have to pay him whatever he wanted this time. I needed the exposure. I'd still have the five pieces he didn't know existed. I could do another show, one that would make even more bank.

JAKE

Last Week of October

Sleep would not touch me that night. Damien dragged me out to Astro Burger at about one o'clock or something, which was a nice distraction. But when we got back to the hotel, he passed out, leaving me alone with my guilt and anxiety. The old familiar nausea had returned.

What could Patrick possibly do to me with all the people around me all the time? What could Fawlty do? I reasoned with myself until I actually started to believe there was nothing anyone could do. I came up with a motto, a mantra, which I'd repeat in my head right up until show time: *'No one can touch me. I am super cool, nobody's fool.'* I was untouchable.

The days leading up to my debuts are a blur of dancing, sweating, sneaking, and slick nausea. Damien was totally out of control. The elusive high he sought belonged to me alone, and it didn't come from pharmaceuticals. My friend had given up the potency of stardust for the cheap thrills of the old neighborhood. He threw it all away for that one stupid chick, too. I'd learn from his mistakes, show him what he could have been.

The preparations for my first performance obliterated all the vulture-like what-ifs that circled my bizarre life. I lost myself in the music and showmanship and adoration. I was on a celebrity binge. I had reached a kind of blissful blackout state. Its power was awesome.

Damien screamed from the bathroom, interrupting my thoughts. The bats were trying to eat his eyeballs again.

Time for another dose.

I tapped on the door. "Damien? Open the door, bud."

"The bats, they're here, they want my eyes. Please, don't let them..."

I tried the doorknob. It didn't turn, so I tapped again.

"The bats are scratching at the door! Do you hear them?"

The unmistakable and familiar edge of panic colored his hoarse voice.

"Damien, I can chase the bats away, but you have to unlock the door."

I was the voice of reason. Me. Ha! Can you imagine being so insanely fucked up that you thought bats were trying to attack you in your own bathroom, and a creep like me was coming to the rescue?

Damien reminded me of that kid who thought he was a pitcher of orange juice. Jeez. Not even I, Master of Pop, Bad Ass of Boy Bandland, MC Fucking McCool, could fix that.

I heard a click, and the door cracked open. I pushed it and saw Damien half-sitting, half-lying on the floor, stringy hair framing his gaunt sweaty face. Scratches bled at the corners of his glassy eyes. He looked up at me. He was no idol. He was a completely wasted fiend in need of salvation, and I was his only potential redeemer. Though, I wasn't into playing savior.

"Take it easy, man," I said. "I'll get the bats out. I've got some medicine right here."

I pulled an Altoids box out of my pocket and flicked it open. I selected three capsules and knelt down next to Damien.

A figure darkened the bathroom doorway, making me jump.

"Sasha," I said.

He looked at Damien, then shifted his gaze to me. I wanted to speak, but I didn't have any words for him. My mouth just kind of hung open as our eyes locked. Damien shoved the capsules in his mouth and asked for water. Sasha gave him a final sweep with his eyes and left the room, pulling the door shut behind him.

"You're still doing that to him?" Sasha asked me when I stepped out of the bathroom.

I said nothing. I helped myself to a Coke from the mini bar and dropped into the sofa.

"Listen, Jake," Sasha said, easing himself into a chair opposite me. "You don't need to do that anymore."

He knew? I wondered for how long. I gave him a sideways stare, playing it cool. He took a deep breath and blew it out.

"I know you've been in tough position here. We did what we had to do, is all. I hope, on some level, you understand. Before we picked you up, Damien was absolutely off his rocker, boasting about how he killed that little girl. I think what pushed him over edge was knowing you saw him and what that could mean. It could be end of not only his career — I don't think he gave shit about that, at that time — but also end of band, and he knew that he'd damaged you. He wanted badly to make things right, but there was no way to do. And I... I thought best thing would be to just get rid of you."

Tears shone in Sasha's eyes.

I almost laughed because he was almost crying, not about wanting to kill me, but about almost not recognizing my commercial potential. He nearly destroyed what would become his biggest meal ticket yet. I kept quiet. I wanted to hear what else he had to say. After what seemed like about an hour, he continued.

"Damien is no threat to you, John." I bristled at hearing my real name. "He's lost. He knows he will never be same as he was before all this shit. He fucked up big time, but, you know he did right by you."

He looked at me with a 'get it?' kind of expression.

"Okay, well, maybe not in kidnapping, but..." he sighed." John, in his mind, he's giving you the world on a fucking silver platter. You understand?"

He looked at me, waiting for a response.

"Yeah, I know," I said. "He really fucked me up, though, man."

Sasha considered this for a minute, studying my face.

"Did he?" he finally said. "Did he really?"

Did he really? That was the million dollar question, wasn't it? As a parade of nightmarish images of Patrick and Mary flashed through my mind, Damien emerged from the bathroom.

"Hey, guys," he croaked. "Is it time to go yet?"

"Go, where, Damien?" Sasha asked, turning toward the ghost of the boy he'd led to fame.

"To school."

He spoke in the soft tone of a feverish six-year-old. I felt a pang of pity for my lost friend. But eclipsing that was the tingle of victory and a powerful surge of ego.

This whole show was mine now.

Mine.

Gone was the shy weed-peddling peeping Tom ghetto boy. In his place, Jake Wolfram stood ready to assume the mantle of postmodern Pop Star. Fuck Damien. He put me here. Fuck Fawlty, too. I was in control.

As soon as Sasha put Damien to bed and took off, there was a knock on the door. I pulled it open and found my old friend Grissom standing there, badge in his hand. Great.

"Hey, officer, you need another autograph?"

He smiled. "Maybe, but I need to have a little chat with you first. It's probably nothing, but I have to at least show my face here. May I come in?"

"Sure," I said, stepping aside.

I followed him over to the couch.

"Have a seat. You want a Coke or anything?"

It was the first time I'd been sober when he showed up.

"No, thanks," he said, sitting down. "I just want to touch base with you regarding this whole art show thing. I saw it in the paper, the ad for the opening."

"Yeah, you're welcome to come. Bring your daughter. Shoot, bring the whole famdamnly."

Grin and wink. So unlike the old me, but, oh, so right for the new and improved me.

"So, that artwork is yours, right?"

"Yes, sir," I lied. "Made it with my own two hands. You should see it. You want a sneak preview? We can go down to the gallery — they're already setting up."

I held my breath and hoped he'd say no.

"Nah, I'll be at your reception; there's no need to make a special trip right now."

Whew.

The cop stood up and extended his hand.

"Sorry to bother you, Mr. Wolfram. It's just a matter of crossing the t's and all that. Good luck with your exhibit and your concert. I'll see you at both."

I shook his hand and showed him to the door.

SASHA

Last Week of October

Cha-ching! This skinny little bastard is fucking gold mine. And I wanted to kill him. Shit, Damien looks like fucked out old whore compared to this kid.

Damien — Jeff, I mean, Jeff was fun for a while, but, come on, after the shit storm, what good is he? He can't even think straight. Not that thinking was in job description, but, you know, I don't need drooling idiot. Way too hard to sell.

But this John... Heh heh heh. Kid after my own fucking heart. He's making lemonade by ocean-full, you know what I am saying? I didn't even know he had art going on. That increases net worth of his — not to mention mine, exponentially.

Now, if I can talk him into signing new contract, I'll be set for life. That private island down in Turks and Caicos is mine as soon as kid can move some CDs and downloads. I must find a way to keep him from looking too close at fine print. He's a smart fuck. A lot smarter than the rest of little pricks.

I got contingency plan, though. He finds out about fake companies I set up to act as In Dreams 'suppliers and contractors,' I'll just cut him in. With token percentage, of course. With earnings siphoned off his own art sales. Brilliant! He'll understand, this kid.

I can tell by what he's done to Damien.

JAKE

Wednesday, October 31

The morning of my debut, I woke up early and had a Town Car take me over to the Staples Center. I was surprised by the number of crew people already there, humping equipment in from a fleet of semi-trucks parked out back. I flashed my laminate and walked through the back door. People jammed the concrete corridors, wearing headsets and wrestling amps and speaker cabinets toward the stage. Either nobody noticed me, or maybe they just didn't care that I was there. I grabbed a banana off of a craft services table and wandered out to the stage.

Thousands of empty seats stretched out for miles in all directions. For the first time, I thought about performing in front of thousands of people. Completely surreal. It made me feel like puking. I wondered what a panic attack felt like and how many I'd already suffered in the past couple of months. It struck me that I had — gasp — a career! That freaked me out even more.

I got the hell out of the building and found my car.

"Hey, take me over to Gallery 551, on Pico."

◇ ◇ ◇

Fawlty flitted around, humming a tune, setting up. Tarps formed geometric ghosts around the perimeter of the space. He turned around to see me peeking under one of the white sheets.

"Jake, welcome. We're just about set for tonight. I'm expecting at least two hundred, maybe just a few more. Lots of RSVPs and VIPs, lots of interest in you," he said, crossing the room to drape his frail arm around my shoulders, pinching my cheek. "It's a shame Patrick won't be able to attend."

He laughed like a fiend, raising goosebumps on my arms. The fucking weasel. I hated him.

Having seen more than enough, I beat it back to the sanctuary of the hotel.

◇ ◇ ◇

Damien was particularly lucid, which was a good thing. I couldn't have dealt with another one of his freak-outs, since I was busy with my own.

"John," he said. "Can we talk about something?"

He was lying on the couch with the drapes pulled. His voice shook ever so slightly through the murk.

"Sure, Damien, what's up?"

I flicked on a lamp. He threw an arm over his eyes.

"I want you to know something, okay? I want you to know that I never meant to hurt you."

He slid his arm up to the top of his head, pulling his overgrown hair back.

Too late.

I wanted to punch him in the mouth. Instead, I gritted my teeth and plopped down in the chair across from him.

"Man, I don't give a shit about that chick, you know? I killed somebody. Big fucking deal. What, I'm supposed to go around being all sad and melancholy forever now?"

He paused, like I was going to say yes. He rubbed his eyes and sat up.

"I am so sorry for all these colossal fuck-ups I caused you, though. And I don't know what to do to feel normal again, to feel like me. I had it all, and now..."

Tears dripped off of his jaw line, making dark dots on his jeans.

I wanted to hug him.

I loathed him.

"John, I want you to have a good life. I know you never got to be a normal kid, with your dad taking off and your mom being... how she is. And I know I really messed you up. I was your friend, and I fucked you over. I was a total dick. I'm trying to make it better. Do you see that? I want you to live the dream, kid. Be a rock star, live the life, try to forget, okay? Please be happy."

I didn't say anything. I looked at the floor while he wiped his eyes. How could I ever forget? Yeah, he gave me an escape from the misery that my life would have become, but at what price?

Our Hallmark moment was interrupted by yet another knock on the door (it felt like someone was forever knocking). Damien opened the door, and the rest of the band flowed into the room. Sasha brought up the rear, holding a sweating magnum of champagne, breaking the absolutely-no-drinking-before-a-show rule (unintentionally setting the tone for the whole tour). Everyone was all smiles and handshakes, happy to finally be back to work.

Reggie came up to me, grabbed me in a playful headlock, and said, "Kid, we brought you a present."

Alex brought in a big rectangular package from the hallway. Reggie steered me over to the couch and put the long box across my lap. I looked at everyone and pulled the bow off with a grin. A wheat colored guitar case held a shiny new, made in the U.S.A. Stratocaster. The deep blue finish put Billy's trademark ring to shame.

"You earned it, kid," Billy said to me with a lascivious wink and lick of the lips.

Ew. But I was touched anyway.

"Take us to the top, dude," Scotty said, clapping me on the back.

I didn't know what to say, so I just grinned like a moron and said thanks, thanks a lot.

Damien stood off to the side, looking at the floor, wiping his nose on his shirt sleeve.

JAKE

Wednesday, October 31

As my vehicle glided to a halt, I checked the mirror one last time, ran a hand through my sticky brush cut. Totally unprepared for this battle, I steadied my breathing and assumed my calmest façade. I told myself there was no danger, no threat to my safety, not with this many witnesses. I pulled on my Revo shades, my Armani flak jacket. Zero hour. Deep breath. Smile. Let's do this.

A neutral party wearing a drive-thru headset and all black crept up to my door, jerked it open, and spoke my name into the bud of his microphone.

Then, I was in it.

As soon as my Chuck Taylor touched the plush red runner, they were on me. An over-zealous firing squad on an AWOL private. Photographic assassins pointed their weapons, commanding my attention from all sides. The syndicate of snipers crouched along the red river, Nikon weapons poised and ready. Camera flashes ignited the violet vellum sky, fire from the muzzles of a hundred assault rifles. Celebrities, picked off in mid-lie, advanced from dark tinted personnel carriers to the neon-framed portal of Gallery 551.

The rush from a crack pipe hits you within seven seconds of inhalation. I can attest to that, firsthand. I can also tell you that's a freaking eternity, compared to this.

"Jake, on your left!" *Flash.*

"Hey, Jake!" *Flash.*

"Smile, kid!" *Flash.*

"Hey, artist, to the right!" *Flash.*

Flash.

Flash.

Flash.

Surrounded, I was forced to surrender. I raised my hands above my head and submitted to their lenses with an air of resignation.

Okay, you got me.

I fucking loved it. I was blinded by the supernova flash bursts, but I loved it. Masses of people waved at me, jumping up and down, screaming from behind the phalanx of *paparazzi.* Not just people — *fans!* Blue and white floaters swam across my field of vision with every blink. Totally surreal. My head swelled with every squeal of my name. My anxiety dissolved to dizzy euphoria. It was beyond intense.

The celebrity high is instantaneous. Not even mainlining hits you that fast or hard. Heroin never felt as smooth. The world whirled around me in a slow motion hallucination of high powered admiration. My skin flushed with a warm tingle from my toes all the way to my scalp. My heart beat like the trance rhythm at an overcrowded rave, yet I felt calm, bordering on numb. I floated along on a sea of serene reverie. No needle required.

Through the glare of my brand new brilliance, I couldn't quite make out what she looked like, but I spotted this chick moving through the crowd. Her inky silhouette stalked me as I drifted across the savage firing range. A dull finger of concern dimpled the bubble of my ecstasy.

Flash.

She moved a beat faster than me.

Ah, just another photographer looking for a place to get a better shot. Don't sweat it, I told myself.

But, I couldn't help sweating it. She moved with precision and purpose, searching for a particular location, predicting the trajectory of my forward motion. Maybe she wanted an autograph. Or my phone number. Sweet. I wondered if she was hot.

Flash.

"Hey, Jake, over here!" I snapped back to my surreal reality.

What the hell, they deserved it, these grunts with cameras. They'd probably been camped out on the sidewalk since early morning. I stopped and gave my best cooler-than-you sneer. I put my head on a slow right to left swivel, giving them all an equal opportunity to capture the money shot.

Flash, flash, flash.

They ate that shit right up.

Okay, so did I. It was a true symbiotic relationship, self-feeding, self-sustaining. I wished it could last forever.

An edge of dread bled through, though, damaging my high. I was no coward, but, well... *he* could be in there. Waiting for me just inside the door. Or in the bathroom, or something. I hadn't given it much thought until I saw that weird chick pacing me. I mean, security was pretty tight, so everything should be fine, but, still, I wasn't a hundred percent.

That chick, my harbinger of horror, perched at the bottom of the steps, right behind the velvet rope. She was a teenager, like me, maybe a year or two older. Damn, she wasn't hot. A bird's nest of frizzy yellow hair floated around her pudgy harsh face. The buttons down the front of her black shirt strained to contain the bloated mess within. I did not see a camera. Was that a dog collar around her neck?

The dog collar?

No way. Couldn't be — could it? Christ, I was freaking myself out. *Just a kid trying to get an eyeful. Get a grip, dickhead.* But, I knew it was her — the girl I'd seen in my hotel room. The one who'd left me the letter. The cousin. The girl from the Megastore! The budding dread I'd felt before fully flowered in the pit of my stomach.

Flash.

I crept up to the velvet rope, struggling to maintain my

celebrity swagger. The weird chick gripped a Starbucks cup in her porky fist. She pulled it back as flashbulbs reflected off the cup's cool white skin, glinted off her sparkly sapphire ring.

Flash.

Warm, thick, sticky liquid slapped my cheek, oozed down my neck, trailed down my leather jacket. It was not latte.

The chick disappeared.

My career was officially launched.

Flash.

It occurred to me that people were photographing me with what looked like blood running down my face. I hurried up the steps and into the gallery. Fawlty greeted me with a champagne flute filled with milk. Give me a break — it was my fucking opening. Couldn't I at least have one stupid glass of champagne? What planet were these people on?

"Oh, my, someone get this boy a towel," he said to no one in particular.

A cloth napkin was thrust into my hand just as someone used another to blot my face. My mom appeared through the parted crowd.

"Hi, mom," I said, drinking my milk.

I wasn't bothered by the shit that girl threw on me. No big. I had premieres to do.

"Let me clean you up, honey," she slurred.

She had either gotten there early or had discovered the mini fridge in the limo that I sent to pick her up. Oh, well, I loved her, and it was good to see her. I put my arm around her shoulders and complimented the designer evening gown Sasha had thoughtfully rented for her.

I waded through the crowd, grinning sheepishly, uttering my thanks to the back-clappers and hand-shakers.

Grissom showed up, as promised. I spied him in a corner with a young lady of maybe ten, who was sipping a soda. I walked over and thanked them for coming. The young lady was indeed his daughter, and I signed one of my slick programs for her, a brochure with my name on it, not Patrick's. She blushed a deep red and wouldn't look at me. I knew how she felt. Some of my heroes were there, too, and I was too shy to approach them.

People in evening attire milled around the gallery, sipping champagne, eating some kind of fancy appetizer things, and oohing and aahing at the fiendish installation pieces. I felt a devilish glee at the thought of them making such a fuss over genuine pieces of poor old Mary. Some of them would pay tens of thousands of dollars for the privilege of housing any one of her parts. It was positively, supremely, ghoulish, and I got a rush off of it that I had never gotten from drugs or spying or anything. It was a brand new delicious and dizzying high. I was instantly addicted.

Scotty, Reggie, Alex, Billy, and Damien stood in a group, marveling at a sculpture that featured a porcupine of decking screws drilled into pelvic bone.

I looped my arm through my mom's as Fawlty approached and pulled me towards an unassuming podium at the center of the gallery. That fucker. I had the contract for the show in my pocket. I never signed it, and he had forgotten to ask me for it. Too bad.

"Good evening, everyone, and thank you for coming to Jake Wolfram's premier exhibition," Fawlty said into the microphone, "I'm sure it will be the first of many spectacular and engaging shows."

Applause.

Mom tugged my arm, and I suddenly felt hot and embarrassed. I noticed my band mates gaping at me like I had two heads or something. They had known about the exhibit for a couple of days, but they'd never asked me any questions or anything. I didn't really think they'd show up at the reception, not with a sound-check to do in an hour's time, but there they were, backing me up.

"Hi," I said from behind the podium. "Um, ever since I was a little kid, I always wanted to be an artist. I always carried around my little notebook full of doodles, made little macaroni sculptures, even painted my bedroom walls with spaghetti sauce once — sorry, Mom."

I looked over at Mom.

She smiled with her eyes full of pride.

I don't think I'd ever made her proud before. It was a bizarre sensation.

"Um, the inspiration for the pieces here...," I continued, "Um... See, Patrick Salinger used to be my neighbor."

As if on cue, a low buzz grew out of the rapt crowd.

I became faintly aware of some shuffling towards the front of the gallery, directly ahead of me.

"We didn't live too far from here, actually," I said above the buzz. "And, um, I used to follow him around, wanting to learn from him and stuff."

Expectant and quizzical faces gazed back at me from the crowd. Was I missing something? Was I talking loud enough? I was speaking English, I thought.

"Well, uh, when Patrick... um, disappeared... uh... and I read about what he'd done..."

It was freaking me out. People whispered to each other and sneaked looks at the front door behind them. Something was wrong.

"I guess it's not very original, but I kind of snagged his concept, and I worked up some pieces of my own that expressed my shock at what he was..."

My voice broke off, and I stared in shock, suddenly zeroing in on the source of distraction.

"You little son of a bitch."

Patrick did not even try to hide the rage in his voice. Nor did he try to hide the gun he pointed directly at my head. How embarrassing would it have been to start bawling right then?

"That work is mine. It's all mine. This is *my* show, not

his."

People looked from him to me, like they were at Wimbledon or some fucking thing. My stomach twisted, and my heart skipped.

"That little fuck got everything that should have been mine. I've been watching that sycophant. He sucked the life out of Damien — look at him."

Everyone turned their eyes to Damien, who was standing about ten feet from me.

"Damien Tungsten, former teen idol. That's right, *former*. There's shit about him that you people would be pretty fucking surprised to know."

Damien looked like he'd been caught with his pants down. I recognized the look from that awful night that seemed like ages before, the night that had brought us to this very moment, when he stood on those steps and saw me in the window.

"And now that little son of a bitch," Patrick continued, pointing his gun at me, "has the balls to leech off my fucking dream."

He flicked the gun to his right, and a vitrine burst with a pop and a gush. Shards of glass sprayed the crowd. Screams filled the cavernous white space of the gallery. Men shoved women to the floor and shielded them with the polyester armor of their tuxedos. Champagne flutes hit the floor in slow motion, bouncing and shattering with a musical tinkling. Patrick shot another sheet of glass, fracturing it into an intricate spider's web, damaging the delicate tissues of Mary Bellows within. The pressure of the liquid inside the tank pushed the web of glass outward, spilling everything onto the glittering wet floor.

Patrick screamed and squeezed off two blind shots as Grissom, and a couple of other security guys or cops or whatever jumped on top of him.

One of the stray bullets hit Fawlty. In the forehead. His eyes glazed over as he crashed to the floor.

A woman screamed.

I saw someone punch Patrick in the side of the face. His mouth gaped in a weird diagonal, blood spilled from one corner.

I shut my eyes and opened them again, hoping a different scene would appear.

People stood up, crying and bathed in champagne.

I wondered if the little cuts they all seemed to have stung from the booze.

They all turned toward Patrick and the cops, watching the struggle to disarm the nutcase they all recognized from the news.

I didn't notice at the time, but the paparazzi went into total overdrive the second Patrick showed up. I would later see pictures of him strolling up the red carpet, smiling and holding his gun up in a wave. Smiling. No shit. There were pictures of him inside, screaming at me, shooting the place up, being taken down, bleeding on the floor, in handcuffs. It was totally fucking unreal.

And, you know what? I was totally fucking *elated*! What a fucking *hyooge* publicity stunt! Ask me about the sales that were generated that night. Go on, ask. Through the motherfucking roof! And I didn't have to so much as split a single cent with that fucking weasel, Fawlty. He was dead! Didn't have to worry about that contract after all! Ha!

"Hey, guys, what do you say we head over to the Staples Center?" I said to the band as soon as Patrick was escorted out through the front door.

Billy and Alex gave me kind of a strange look. Then we all looked at each other. No one was hurt, but we were all pretty wigged out. A couple of the guys were pale and shaking. We were all for getting out of there.

Grissom pulled me aside as I was about to climb into the Navigator.

"Jesus, Jake, that was something, huh?"

He scanned my face pretty intensely.

I tried my best to look shocked and sick.

"I think everything's going to be okay, but I'll be in

touch. I won't be at the concert because I have a desk-load of paperwork to do because of what happened here, but I'll be watching you. You okay?"

I wasn't exactly sure what he meant by watching me. Did he mean that he was my new biggest fan? Or did he think I was suspicious or something? Maybe he knew the art wasn't mine. Anyway, I was way too high on adrenaline to give a rip, so I just smiled and nodded as I closed myself into my vehicle.

I couldn't wait to hit the stage. Epinephrine surged through my body like a tidal wave. Unlike the rest of the quavering band, I was all smiles.

JAKE

Wednesday, October 31

An absolute flood of people swarmed the arena's entrances, sending a shock wave of excited nausea through my manic being.

"Wow, all those people are here to see us?" I asked, totally awestruck.

I sounded like such a kid. I couldn't help it. I thought two hundred people wanting to see 'my' art was amazing. This was something else. Way better than heroin.

"Not only do they want to see us, Jakey boy, they want to scream in our faces and rip every shred of clothing from our bodies," Scotty said with gravity and something approaching boredom.

His angular face was still pale.

"The magic happens, though," Damien said, "when every mouth in the house is singing words that came straight from my head. I give their lives meaning, I put their wants, needs, fears, frustrations into words in ways that they can't."

The other guys exchanged eye rolls at Damien's musing. He didn't seem to notice. He was lost in his own world. And even though his words were those of some kind of egomaniac, his tone was one of a man defeated. He sounded as if he was trying to let go of something, some former self, a former life, maybe.

When we got to the dressing rooms, Damien pulled me aside.

"Dude, that was some sick shit you made."

He smoothed his hair, preening in the lighted mirror in front of him.

"It looked just like some of Patrick's stuff that was in the paper. When the fuck did you have the time to do that?"

"Yeah. I don't know, man."

I didn't feel like talking about it. I was beginning to get nervous about all those people waiting for us. I was also starting to realize that I could have been killed less than an hour ago. Oh, well, the show must go on, right?

"Did Patrick really make stuff like that out of that girl?"

Damien stroked his eyebrows with an index finger, checked his teeth. I didn't believe he wanted the answer to that question. I wasn't prepared to tell him the truth, anyway, and couldn't figure out why he was asking me.

"How would I fucking know, Damien?"

I pulled some pills from my pocket, then opted for the white powder instead.

"Here, this'll keep you up, man."

"Hey, um... You think I'm, you know, washed up now, like Patrick said back there?" His brown eyes leaked. "I know things are bad, man."

Desperation was so ugly on him.

I shrugged and offered him a couple of fat lines cut on a little square mirror, just like we were actors in *Saturday Night Fever* or some other corny old drug movie. He snorted, licked his teeth, grinned at me. I felt bad for him.

Well, not really.

"Hey, guys," Sasha called from the doorway, "show time."

We donned our headsets, prompting my 'you want fries with that' joke, and stood at the side of the stage. I saw the sea of people through a break in the curtain. A wave of sheer terror hit me like a train. It must have registered on my face because Reggie put his hand on my shoulder and told me I'd be okay.

"This is it, kid," Damien said to me. We had a group hug and the band shouted "In Dreams" in unison, then broke.

I found my gaffer's tape 'X' towards the back of the stage and planted my feet on either side of it. The curtain flew up, immersing us in a flood of bright hot light vibrating with shrill screams. It was shocking and scary and unbelievable and exhilarating and supremely amazing. When we sounded our first acapella "aaaaaaaaah" to begin 'It's You,' the entire building jumped and shook.

We did about six or seven songs without incident. I could not believe I was up on the stage, dancing and singing (okay, lip-synching) with In Dreams. I was overcome with absolute ecstasy.

And then Damien fell.

JAKE

Wednesday, October 31 —

Wednesday, November 7

The doctors over at Cedars-Sinai said it was some kind of cardiac hiccup. Then, they tested Damien's urine and found evidence of cocaine use. Further examination proved that Damien had suffered a heart attack as a direct result of inhaling 'a copious amount' of cocaine. Oops.

After Damien collapsed on stage, our sound guy scrambled to come up with three songs on which Damien did not sing lead. We blew through those songs, fought our way to a limo, and sped off to the hospital.

I had an absolutely amazing time. Not one single screwup in my dance steps or anything. I was totally bummed that I didn't get to hook up with a groupie, though. So much for the best night of my life.

Damien was sleeping when we finally got in to see him. Like I said, he'd had a coke-induced heart attack. What is the show biz code word for said event? You guessed it: 'exhaustion.' That's the word Sasha gave the media, too, as we all filed into Damien's private room. It's the same word you hear every time this happens to a big star. Now you know, they are either in the hospital for drug-related heart problems, are so depressed they've tried to off themselves, or they're headed to rehab. The doctors wanted to keep our boy to run some tests, so I guess they thought things were at least a little bit serious.

Billy, Reggie, Alex, Scotty, Sasha, and I were shown to

a private waiting room, where we could wait for Damien to wake up without the press hounding us. The guys congratulated me on a great night, and we all said what a fucked up but exciting ride it had been. Then we talked about our schedule and what our strategy would be now that Damien was on the bench.

Sasha placed the burden squarely on my shoulders.

"Jake, we got four days before our next show. You ready for this?"

I didn't know what he was talking about, but I was up for just about anything. I was on top of the world. My hands still shook from the adrenaline that surged through my circulatory system.

"You guys let me know what you think of this plan, okay?" Sasha said, looking around. "Damien has been our leader since beginning. With him out of commission for at least a couple of shows, we need to get into studio and re-record some of the bigger songs, so his voice isn't on there. We need new lead guy. You up for it, Jake?"

They all looked at me. No way. Was he serious? My eyes widened. Of course I was up for it. And I told them so in no uncertain terms. Hell, yeah!

The following four days were spent in the recording studio, re-mixing In Dreams' big hits. Damien's vocals were scrubbed, and mine were laid down in their place. I was the star. It was that easy.

Flash.

Damien stayed in the hospital. Sasha and I went to tell him the band's plan after my recording sessions.

Damien sat in his bed, oxygen tube up his nose, watching *Wheel of Fortune* as Sasha and I strode into his hospital room.

"Hey, buddy," I leered, "the nurses treating you alright in here?"

I winked at him, smirking at his misfortune. A weak smile was his only reply. His eyes burned into me with an unspoken ferocity. I looked away and took a seat in one of the scratchy orange chairs.

"Damien," Sasha gushed. "It's good to see you sitting up."

He hugged Damien and pumped his hand.

"We've got some good news, boy."

A young nurse came in and left a big Styrofoam cup with a bendy straw sticking out of the top on Damien's bedside table. Her broad smile told me that she was an In Dreams fan. Her fat ass told me that I needed new fans.

"Damien," Sasha continued, pulling a chair up to the side of the bed. "Listen," he said, turning to me.

"Hey, Jake, can you shut that thing off?" he asked, pointing to the TV.

I walked over and pushed the power button.

"Listen, Jeff, we are so sorry you're stuck in this place."

He grabbed Damien's hand and held it for a second.

"But, we gotta get back out on road, you know? You pulled first disappearing act and derailed the tour — we just can't afford to do it again. There's no way band could survive that."

Damien's moist eyes scalded my face. I knew then that he hated me as much as I hated him. Oh, well, that's show biz. Fucking idiot. This whole thing was his own goddamn fault, anyway.

He was definitely not thrilled with me standing in as lead. You could tell by the seething look on his face. He never said a word the whole time Sasha was telling him how things were going to go down. He didn't have the strength to argue. He was detoxing on top of having all these weird heart tests.

Damien, to me, looked sweaty and hollow and scared and more than a little irate. He had a weird smell. It was one that I had a little trouble placing, but I definitely knew what it was. It wasn't until we were on stage in Seattle that I finally remembered where I had smelled it before — Mary. Damien smelled like decomposition.

I wondered where the guy's parents were, or if he even had any.

JAKE

November — May

Being a rock star on tour was an awesome combination of freedom and imprisonment, wealth and poverty, popularity and loneliness. Only two weeks into it, I was dog tired. Wrapping a show at eleven o'clock, partying until three, getting up at noon, traveling to the next town, then setting up all over again was a total grind. Sasha had to know where I was every second. I couldn't go shopping or to McDonald's or anything, just like when I was with Patrick and then Damien. All I could do was hang out with the other guys in our hotel or bus. You get real close to the other guys in your band, but, fuck, you can't get away from them when you need a break.

At the end of the second week, I had a shadow, too. Sasha had worked a book deal for me, so I had this ghostwriter following me around for a couple of weeks, documenting everything I ate, drank, smoked, and fucked. That was exhausting, too, but I can't wait for my 'autobiography' to hit the shelves. I've already got a book signing lined up for after our tour wraps.

I had my mom fly into Boston and join the tour about three weeks into it. She was doing a lot better, living in a real house, laying off the booze, starting up my fan club. My new career had given her a second chance, and it wasn't wasted on her. She flourished, acting like the whole band's mom, making sure we ate our veggies and brushed our teeth. It was the dysfunctional family that I never had, and I loved it.

Damien, my lost brother, fought a different battle back in L.A. Sasha told us that he had contracted some kind of infection, endocarditis or something, I think. He'd gotten it after he'd had some test where they put wires in your veins or something — angioplasty, maybe. The dude was in bad shape.

We sent him teddy bears wearing lingerie and balloon bouquets and shit like that, but I don't know if he ever even got them.

And then we heard that Damien was discharged from the hospital and went missing. Rumors circulated that he'd OD'ed in the bathroom of some sleazy bar in North Hollywood. Good riddance.

The rumors died down, and I found that the less I heard of him, the more I could forget about the whole Mary Situation. He was likely dead, and that part of my life was over.

Well, okay, that's not quite true, since 'my art' had really taken off, and people were actually buying the shit I had broken out of storage after that first fiasco of a show. It was crazy. The old Bull's Eye piece sold for something like seventeen grand. Unreal. I was doing some drawing, but just little sketches. There was no way I could have kept track of a whole paint set or anything on the road, so I stuck to woodless graphite and an eleven by fourteen sketchbook. I was planning a real exhibit of my drawings for the following summer. I wanted to hook up with some other artist-musicians and have one of those big celebrity art shows.

Patrick was in jail. He had been charged with first degree murder and a lot of other shit. I let out a huge sigh of relief every night as I watched Nancy Grace. There was never any mention of my involvement beyond being that psychotic fuck's neighbor and my being held hostage or whatever. My old friend Grissom made a lot of guest appearances on that show, but he never talked about me for some reason. It turned out that Patrick would never face trial because he was proven criminally insane by some high-profile psychiatrist. He was a certified nut job. Shit, I could have told them that. He screamed about how all that art was his, all his, and I was this greedy sycophant, stealing everyone's dreams (well, okay, that part wasn't too far off the mark). He finally got some big name journalist to help him write an article detailing how he made the installation pieces. Psycho.

While his life was going to shit in a very public way, I negotiated with a couple of record labels. I played them against each other in an unreal bidding war. They took me to five-star restaurants, sent me tons of clothes and gifts, and one even bought me a brand-new BMW motorcycle, even though I didn't have my driver's license yet. Each of them tried their damnedest to get me nailed down. One finally did. I got a five album, hundred-million dollar deal. No shit, a hundred million! There were a lot of contingencies on that astronomical number, though. I had to meet ever-increasing sales quotas and shit with each new release. And I had to stay off drugs and out of rehab.

I moved the last of my shit out of the Laurel Canyon house on a break halfway through our tour. I was supposed to live there with the other guys, but Sasha changed his mind and said I should have a place of my own, being the band leader with a solo deal and all. So I leased one of F. Scott Fitzgerald's old places, just up the hill from my favorite Cajun restaurant on the Strip. It was pretty sweet. It was this huge stucco two-story with one of those tile roofs and an Infinity pool. I was going to have some huge parties in that place. Fuck all those old band rules. I couldn't stick to them from the start. I was going solo.

Hey, none of my new neighbors had curtains, either.

Ha ha. Just kidding. I didn't peep anymore, I learned my lesson about that shit. I told my mom to trash the old telescope when she moved out of the downtown rat trap. She must have disposed of my meth lab, too, but she never said a single word about any of that stuff.

Yep, everything was great.

Sasha said I was gonna be huge, legendary.

And I was.

DETECTIVE O'BRIEN, L.A.P.D.

(aka, GRISSOM)

Sunday, May 12

He seemed like a real nice kid. I hated to see him go down like that. My daughter was heartbroken. Again. Second time by this In Dreams band. Fucking idiots. But it is what it is. We knew all about his art projects. Come on, give us a little credit. We tested all that shit that Salinger shot up at the art gallery. Sent some of it to the Body Farm, even. The boy may not have killed that little girl, but he had detailed knowledge of what was in those fish tanks. He may have even helped put her there. I don't buy Salinger's story that the kid just sat and watched it all happen. Bullshit. That boy knows a lot more than he's letting on. Smart fuck, that kid, running off and joining the neighbor's band, hiding in the spotlight.

Yes, Salinger maintains that he held the boy hostage and forced him to watch, but that guy's batshit, so who knows? I'll let the courts decide.

As soon as he stepped off that plane, they sped Jake right over to Central Lock Up. Maybe he even got the same cell Robert Blake had. Wouldn't that be ironic? The TV crews were already there, all set to go. I made sure of it, called them myself. I even brought my own little podium to the airport, shoved it in the back seat of my unmarked patrol car. I knew I'd need it for my little press conference. It's about time I get my big break.

He came stumbling out of the jet-way, just like he was staggering down the red carpet on his way to some damn Hollywood premiere. His manager had to hold him up by the arm, he was so intoxicated. He also ruined my shoes with his stinking celebrity puke, the bastard. But we got him. He's no victim, that kid.

I was on Fox News' *On the Record* with Greta that night, some CNN show the morning after. That boy isn't the only one who turned a profit off of that whole mess. Who knows, maybe I'll even get my own show on Fox News. I've already got a multi-million dollar book deal. Everybody wants a piece of the action. True crime is a hot commodity, especially when the players are such high-profile celebrities. It's reality TV to the *n*th power. There is serious cash to be made. Loads and loads of it.

God bless the media.

I'm buying a house in the Bahamas next week.

JAKE

Tuesday, July 9

Okay, yeah, so I got arrested. Big deal. I was in jail for a whole five minutes or something. That Grissom asshole, O'Brien, was waiting to ambush me at LAX, with about forty-five other cops and twenty-seven thousand media douchebags.

"John William Thomas," Grissom said to me with a shit-eating grin as I stepped out of the jet-way, tripping over my backpack. "Son, you're under arrest for obstruction of justice..."

That was all I heard. The buzzing in my head grew and drowned out any further conversation. I was drunk off my ass, and I puked on the cop's shoes. They zipped some plastic garbage bag tie thing on my wrists and hauled me out to a squad car. I threw up in the back seat and had to smell it all the way across town in heavy traffic.

They took my picture, got my autograph, and sat me in an empty room with a two-way mirror on one wall. Sasha bailed me out, and that was that. I was in Central Lock Up for a total of thirty-six minutes. Our lawyer says I'll never be arraigned or anything. I'm an innocent victim. Patrick's testimony — the only 'evidence' against me — doesn't mean shit because he's in the loony bin. Besides, he swears he held me hostage and made me help him anyway. What a douche.

But, the up-side: you know what all the extra media attention brought me? Loads of new fans. All with scads of disposable cash, screaming and crying for me, anxiously awaiting the day they can purchase my very own autobiography.

And that day has arrived.

◇ ◇ ◇

It was the biggest book signing ever at the Burbank Barnes & Noble store.

A huge mob buzzed outside. Someone told me that girls fainted in line, overwhelmed by the mere thought of having their books touched by my hand. What a fucking rush.

Some kind of commotion erupted outside the front door. A limo pulled up. Shit, I wasn't ready for any VIP guests yet — my hair girl hadn't even started. I didn't have my mocha frappuccino.

"Looks like you got an important fan, kid," Sasha said. "Couldn't wait to see you, I guess."

Sasha and I, along with the bookstore manager and my hair dresser, watched the back door of the car swing open. A denim clad pair of legs emerged. A pair of black leather Beatles boots touched the curb. Damien pulled himself out of the doorframe, ignoring the driver who came around to give him a hand.

He wasn't dead?

He wasn't dead.

He looked super thin and so pale. He reminded me of a scarecrow.

A girl emerged, almost unnoticed, behind him. *The* girl. The one from my room, the record store, the steps in front of the gallery! Mary's cousin. With Damien!?

He moved slowly toward the door. A security guard opened it and allowed him to pass while holding back a group of tearful teenagers and blocking Mary's cousin's entrance.

One of the sobbing girls screamed: "Oh, my God, Damien! Tell Jake that I love him!"

Damien glared at her with a hatred that I could feel from halfway across the store.

My old friend shuffled across the mocha colored commercial carpet, his shadow-ringed eyes boring into me.

We all saw it at the same instant, the bookstore manager, the hair dresser, Sasha, and me. One small black circle at the end of a graphite-colored rectangular cylinder.

I felt the impact before I heard the pop.

Time slammed to a halt.

My eyes found a familiar figure in the middle of the store's big plate glass window. Mary's cousin. Kelly. I dimly wondered why the guards hadn't let her in behind Damien. Her hair still looked like a bird's nest. Her hands clapped the sides of her round face, pushing her open mouth into an oval. I couldn't tell whether she looked happy or sad.

My hair dresser jumped off the back of the elevated platform and ran shrieking into the distance behind me. The bookstore manager shouted into her walkie-talkie for someone to call 911, for Christ's sake, it was an emergency! Sasha ducked down behind me, making some weird noise that sounded like "ohmmmm, ohmmmm, ummmmm." A couple of blue uniformed cops rushed through the front doors and tackled Damien from behind.

A replay of Patrick in the art gallery flashed through my mind. Hot blood trickled down my side.

That fucker shot me.

Flash.

About the Author:

S. S. Michaels is a writer of transgressive fiction. She holds degrees in Business Administration and Film & Video Production. She has lived abroad, traveled widely, jumped out of an airplane and driven a race car. In film and television, she read slush and wrote coverage, then moved on to become a production coordinator. She finally served as a TV network financial analyst before leaving Hollywood. She lives with her husband, two kids, and two dogs.

If you enjoyed Idols & Cons, look for Revival House coming 2012 from Omnium Gatherum. http://omniumgatherumedia.com

24086864R00127

Made in the USA
Lexington, KY
05 July 2013